LANGUAGE ARTS
SEVENTEENTH- AND EIGHTI
ENGLISH LITERA

MW01121661

# CONTENTS

| | |
|---|---|
| Author: | **Mary Robbins, M.A.** |
| Editor: | Alan Christopherson, M.S. |
| Illustrator: | Alpha Omega Graphics |

Alpha Omega Publications®

804 N. 2nd Ave. E., Rock Rapids, IA 51246-1759
© MM by Alpha Omega Publications, Inc.   All rights reserved.
LIFEPAC is a registered trademark of Alpha Omega Publications, Inc.

John Bunyan

Oliver Goldsmith

Samuel Johnson

John Milton

Alexander Pope

Jonathan Swift

# SEVENTEENTH- AND EIGHTEENTH-CENTURY ENGLISH LITERATURE

The seventeenth and eighteenth centuries in England may seem far removed from today, but the of history and literature in this LIFEPAC® should illustrate some significant similarities. Many pro that trouble people today existed then. Political corruption and struggles for power were even more com-mon. Wars were being waged often for economic purposes. Cities were becoming industrialized, and the displaced poor were flocking to those cities to find work—and to live in slums. Trade was flourishing, but so were the corrupting attitudes that often accompany wealth. Money was becoming more and more pow-erful while good works and good families counted less. Much of the newly educated reading public lacked a knowledge and appreciation of Greek and Roman literature and encouraged the publication of rapidly written periodicals. Newly built smoke stacks of industry were beginning to produce black clouds of pol-lution. Changes were happening so rapidly that many people felt the same fear of the future that many people feel today. In short, more people were gaining more power and often were not certain what to do with that newly acquired political and economic strength.

The writers of the best literature of those two centuries were involved in their times. They did not with-draw from their responsibilities. They wrote poetry, essays, and longer works specifically to inform the public of the changes taking place and to persuade it to do something about those changes. John Milton wrote essays to support the actions of the Puritan government. He wrote fewer political works after the king's restoration. Yet his concerns were still for other people; his themes in *Paradise Lost* are centered around God's will and man's free will during unsettled times. Similarly, the Puritan John Bunyan wrote about the salvation of a character named Christian so that Christian could serve as an example for read-ers needing such spiritual support. Writing somewhat later, Jonathan Swift chose satire to belittle indi-viduals and practices that represented to him political, moral, and cultural decay. He had been actively involved in his political party's government but was removed from that position by the opposition. Finally, Oliver Goldsmith satirized the greed and foolish political and personal practices of his day, but he also described sympathetically the unfortunate results of the agricultural and industrial revolutions taking place. Since these writers had studied classical literature and all had admired its organization and clarity, they desired to write literature logically organized and convincingly presented with carefully chosen words. They desired to create beautiful works of art—to please as well as to inform.

Because many subjects you will find here are still important issues and because the literature is enjoyable to read, you should benefit both intellectually and spiritually from this study.

## OBJECTIVES

**Read these objectives**. The objectives tell you what you will be able to do when you have successfully completed this LIFEPAC.

When you have completed this LIFEPAC, you should be able to:

1. Describe the political, economic, and cultural background of the seventeenth and eighteenth centuries.

2. Explain the resulting social unrest caused by the rapid political, economic, and cultural changes.

3. Outline John Milton's personal crises and their effect on the themes of his work.

4. Explain Milton's early interest in Christ's role in saving mankind in the poem "On the Morning of Christ's Nativity."

5. Define Milton's own attitude toward his poetic gift and his blindness in his sonnet "On His Blindness."

6. Identify Milton's purpose and his use of epic structure, recurring Biblical types, and imagery in Books I, VIII, and XII of *Paradise Lost*.

7. Outline John Bunyan's biography and emphasize those events that shaped his great work *Pilgrim's Progress*.

8. Identify Bunyan's use of allegory, realistic human traits, and symbols in selections from *Pilgrim's Progress*.

9. Outline the major events in the life of Alexander Pope.

10. Define the methods and forms Pope used in his satire.

11. Outline Jonathan Swift's biography, with emphasis on the political and religious activities that most influenced his satire.

12. Explain Swift's satiric purpose in short passages from *Gulliver's Travels*.

13. Outline the major events in the life and career of Samuel Johnson.

14. Define the literary, moral, and political attitudes of Samuel Johnson.

15. Outline Oliver Goldsmith's writing career and explain some of the aspects of his style.

16. Identify and explain the historical background and sentimentality of Goldsmith's poem *The Deserted Village*.

**Survey the LIFEPAC**. Ask yourself some questions about this study. Write your questions here.

_____

_____

_____

_____

_____

_____

_____

_____

# I. HISTORICAL BACKGROUND

History and literature were closely related during the seventeenth and eighteenth centuries. You should not attempt to study the literature written at that time without having a solid understanding of major political, economic, and cultural developments and their effects. This section explains background events. The charts that are included should help you keep these events in historical perspective.

## SECTION OBJECTIVES

**Review these objectives.** When you have completed this section, you should be able to:

1.  Describe the political, economic, and cultural background of the seventeenth and eighteenth centuries.
2.  Explain the resulting social unrest caused by the rapid political, economic, and cultural changes.

## VOCABULARY

**Study these words** to enhance your learning success in this section.

| | | |
|---|---|---|
| displaced | maneuver | sensibility |
| dissenter | nonconformist | sentimental |
| effeminate | parish | suppressive |
| emigrate | periodical | theme |
| lyrical | propagandist | |

**Note:** All vocabulary words in this LIFEPAC appear in **boldface** print the first time they are used. If you are unsure of the meaning when you are reading, study the definitions given.

# EVENTS 1600-1800

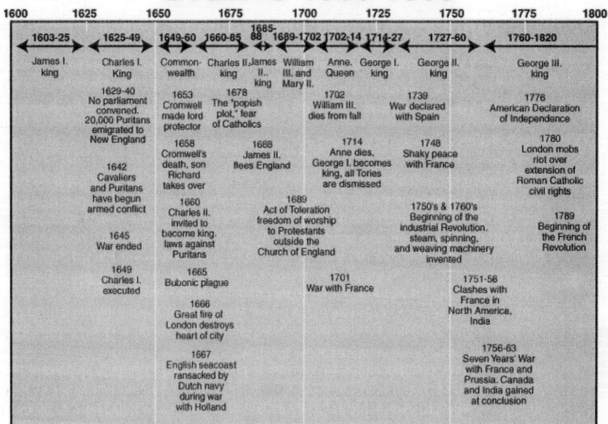

| 1600 | 1625 | 1650 | 1675 | 1700 | 1725 | 1750 | 1775 | 1800 |

**1603-25** | **1625-49** | **1649-60** | **1660-85** | **1685-88** | **1689-1702** | **1702-14** | **1714-27** | **1727-60** | **1760-1820**

**James I.**
king

**Charles I.**
King

1629-40
No parliament
convened.
20,000 Puritans
emigrated to
New England

1642
Cavaliers
and Puritans
have begun
armed conflict

1645
War ended

1649
Charles I.
executed

**Common-
wealth**

1653
Cromwell
made lord
protector

1658
Cromwell's
death, son
Richard
takes over

1660
Charles II.
invited to
become king.
laws against
Puritans

1665
Bubonic plague

1666
Great fire of
London destroys
heart of city

1667
English seacoast
ransacked by
Dutch navy
during war
with Holland

**Charles II.**
king

1678
The "popish
plot," fear
of Catholics

1688
James II.
flees England

**James
II.,
king**

1689
Act of Toleration
freedom of worship
to Protestants
outside the
Church of England

**William
III. and
Mary II.**

1702
William III.
dies from fall

1701
War with France

**Anne.
Queen**

1714
Anne dies,
George I. becomes
king, all Tories
are dismissed

**George I.
king**

**George II.
king**

1739
War declared
with Spain

1748
Shaky peace
with France

1750's & 1760's
Beginning of the
industrial Revolution.
steam, spinning,
and weaving machinery
invented

1751-56
Clashes with
France in
North America,
India

1756-63
Seven Years' War
with France and
Prussia. Canada
and India gained
at conclusion

**George III.
king**

1776
American Declaration
of Independence

1780
London mobs
riot over
extension of
Roman Catholic
civil rights

1789
Beginning of
the French
Revolution

**Chart 1**

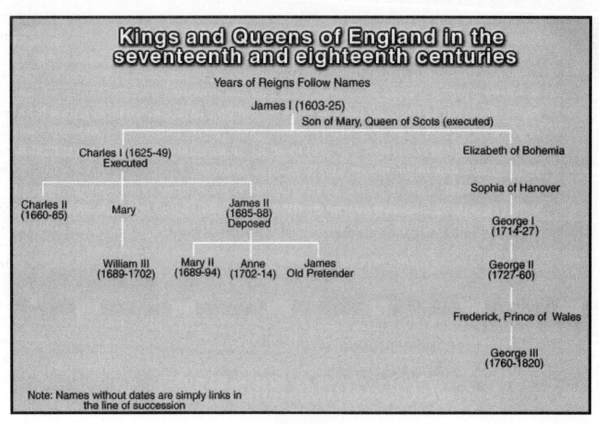

## Kings and Queens of England in the seventeenth and eighteenth centuries

Years of Reigns Follow Names

James I (1603-25)
Son of Mary, Queen of Scots (executed)

Charles I (1625-49)
Executed

Elizabeth of Bohemia

Sophia of Hanover

Charles II
(1660-85)

Mary

James II
(1685-88)
Deposed

George I
(1714-27)

William III
(1689-1702)

Mary II
(1689-94)

Anne
(1702-14)

James
Old Pretender

George II
(1727-60)

Frederick, Prince of Wales

George III
(1760-1820)

Note: Names without dates are simply links in
the line of succession

**Chart 2**

4

## THE COMMONWEALTH AND EARLIER

*Commonwealth* is the term used to describe the Puritans' control of English government from 1649 until 1660. To understand how the Puritans became powerful enough to gain control of England, you must first understand who the Puritans were. The term *Puritan* was probably first applied during Elizabethan times to those men, mostly craftsmen and citizens of the flourishing bourgeois group, who believed that the Church of England should be "purified" of unnecessary ritual that was no longer meaningful and of organization that was no longer able to reach individual members. These **dissenters** resented their government's imposing on them what they considered to be a corrupt faith. **Parish** priests of the Church of England were awarded their positions by the owner of the most land in the area. The clergyman's payment came out of parish tax funds and, once established, was automatic. Once a vicar was given a parish, he almost always kept that parish. The overseeing bishops were appointed by the monarch. Thus, by the time of Elizabeth's successor, James I (see Chart 2), seemingly no division existed between church and state. Tax money supported the church, and the king governed it.

Anglicans, members of the Church of England, feared these Puritans and other dissenters, or **nonconformists**, because they rebelled not only against the church but also against the state, since church and state were so closely related. Fearful Anglicans made laws to enforce conformity to the Church of England. One such law was responsible for John Bunyan's stay in Bedford jail. These laws forced Puritans further away from the party of the king.

James I himself widened that division by insisting on his absolute power as king over the powers of Parliament, which contained several Puritan members. James wished to ally England with Catholic Spain, a wish that further angered the Puritans. His son, Charles I, was so eager to control England without Parliament that no Parliament was convened from 1629 to 1640 (see Chart 1). Moreover, Charles clearly preferred Catholic ritual and began to restore it to the English Church. This period of time was so difficult for the Puritans that nearly twenty thousand **emigrated** to America. In 1640, when the newly convened Parliament refused to give Charles money to quiet unrest in Scotland, the stage was set for the civil war, which began in 1642, between the king's forces (sometimes called Cavaliers or Royalists) and the Puritans (also called Roundheads).

Puritans felt justified in defying the king because they disapproved of the moral degeneration that seemed to originate from the king and his Cavaliers and because they believed in religious and, thus, political democracy. Just as each Puritan felt able to examine his own conscience and to study and interpret the Bible without the aid of clergymen, he also felt the responsibility and competence to play an active part in his government.

In 1645 the Puritans won the civil war. In 1649, after some Puritan **maneuvering** in Parliament, Charles I was executed. Thus, in 1649 the Commonwealth began its eleven year existence. During this period Parliament was the ruling body until 1653 when the Puritan leader of the Parliamentary forces, Oliver Cromwell, was declared Lord Protector. Oliver Cromwell died in 1658. His son could not prevent an invitation to Charles II to return to England as king. By this time most English citizens had become tired of the Puritan government's **suppressive** actions, which included closing theaters by Parliamentary act from 1642 to 1660, beheading the Archbishop of Canterbury, and evicting Anglican clergymen from their parishes. The English were eager to celebrate Charles II's return. Thus in 1660, Charles II was made king and the English monarchy was restored.

5

**Answer these questions.**

1.1 What was the Commonwealth? _____

_____

_____

1.2 Who fought the civil war taking place in 1642 to 1645?_____

_____

_____

1.3 Did the Puritans approve of the close ties between the Church of England and the English government? Why or why not?_____

_____

_____

1.4 What are some reasons why Puritans emigrated to New England?_____

_____

_____

1.5 Why did the Commonwealth come to an end in 1660? _____

_____

_____

### THE RESTORATION OF CHARLES II

The Restoration did not altogether quiet the discontent that had led to civil war. Anglicans still feared Puritan influence, and Puritans as well as many Anglicans feared renewed Catholic pressure from the monarchy. Less important uprisings occurred in 1678, 1685, and finally, in 1688. Even though Charles II had, by his Act of Grace, pardoned those Puritans not directly responsible for Charles I's death, the Cavalier Parliament caused nearly two thousand clergy with Puritan leanings to leave the Church of England in 1661. By 1672 the Test Act forced all officers of the state, civil and military, to prove their sympathies by taking communion according to the form of the Church of England.

Charles I's Catholic preferences had so frightened the English that they readily believed Titus Oates (1649-1705) who invented a "Popish Plot" in which Catholics were supposed to have planned to assassinate Charles II and other political leaders so that they could place his brother James II (a strong Roman Catholic) on the throne. Memories and resentments of previous Catholic injustices were still fresh: Queen "Bloody" Mary I, daughter of Henry VIII, had burned Protestants at the stake only a century earlier; and the Catholic-inspired Gunpowder Plot (when Guy Fawkes was prepared to blow up the king and Parliament) had happened in 1605. Once again this fear, based on the imaginary "Popish Plot," renewed violence; some thirty-five people were executed for supposed treason.

When James II took the throne in 1685 at his brother's death, he confirmed some of those fears. In 1688 he imprisoned seven bishops of the Church of England in the London Tower. When his second wife bore a son, many feared the obvious Catholic heir to the throne.

Fortunately, English Protestants found a solution without the execution of another king. Charles II's elder niece Mary, heiress to the throne, had been contracted to marry William of Orange, of Protestant Holland. William was quickly invited to England to insure Protestantism in 1688. This turn of events caused James and many of his followers, known as Jacobites, to flee to France. William and Mary's acceptance of the throne was known as "The Glorious Revolution." At that time, Parliament was given the power to determine the succession to the throne. That "revolution" provided for political and religious toleration and thus brought government reform agreeable to the English majority.

**Write the letter of the correct answer on the line.**

1.6 What was the Restoration? _____
    a. Oliver Cromwell was restored to the throne.
    b. Charles II was invited back to England to be king.
    c. Charles I was invited back to England to be king.
    d. Order was restored to England in 1688.

1.7 What form of discrimination was not used against the Puritans immediately after the Restoration? _____
    a. Clergymen with Puritan sympathies lost their positions.
    b. All officers of the state were forced by the Test Act to take communion according to the Church of England.
    c. Some Puritans were imprisoned.
    d. Some Puritans were shipped to Africa.

1.8 What is one reason why the English were afraid of a Catholic monarch? _____
    a. Unpleasant memories of "Bloody" Mary, who had burned Protestants at the stake, remained.
    b. Catholic kings had joined England with Italy.
    c. A Catholic king would eliminate the English language.
    d. Catholics had blown up the Parliament once already.

**Answer these questions.**

1.9 Who were the Jacobites? _____

_____

1.10 What was "The Glorious Revolution?" _____

_____

_____

## THE GLORIOUS REVOLUTION TO 1745

When William and Mary were invited to England, Parliament became more powerful. Two political parties, the Tories and Whigs, emerged to struggle for control of Parliament during William's reign. The Tories' ancestors were, supposedly, the Royalists of the earlier seventeenth century. The Whigs' ancestors had been anti-Royalist. The Tories supported the present order of the church and state and were mainly landowners and lower-level clergymen. Whigs usually supported commerce, religious toleration, and Parliamentary reform. These parties, however, were hardly like today's parties; they were more like groups of politicians allied to promote common interests.

William III's twelve-year reign was marked by military matters, a characteristic the Tories were quick to criticize. He quieted Jacobite uprisings in Scotland, subdued Ireland, and conducted a continental war against France to stop her influence and control. William was not popular with the Tories because of his connections with Holland; the Dutch were seen by the English as money-grabbing merchants. The Tory Jonathan Swift satirized the Dutch in Book Three of *Gulliver's Travels* by portraying their merchants stomping on a crucifix to persuade the Japanese to trade with them.

William was killed by a fall from his horse in 1702 and Anne, William's sister-in-law, became Queen until 1714. The Whigs remained in power and continued military activities to boost the economy. The Tories continued to complain until 1710 when they came into power. The Tories finally calmed the war with France. Jonathan Swift became their chief **propagandist**. These years, however, were not calm.

In spite of the Toleration Act of 1689, which permitted Protestant dissenters to hold their own services instead of attending those of the Church of England, the Catholics were still feared. In fact, the threat of the Jacobites and the resulting fears have been compared to the fears of Communism in the Western countries in the 1940s and 1950s. After Anne's death in 1714, the crown went to George I of Hanover, a small kingdom that later became part of Germany (see Chart 2). The Hanover kings, who ruled until 1820, were criticized for their preference for the German language over English, their preference for **effeminate** music and unimportant scholarly matters, and their controversial personal lives. Yet they did bring stability to the throne while tremendous social and economic changes swept the country.

**Answer** *true* **or** *false*.

1.11 _____ The Tories were members of one of two political parties: they had Royalist preferences and supported the church and state already existing.

1.12 _____ The Whigs were members of the other political party; they also had Royalist preferences and usually supported commerce, religious toleration, and Parliamentary reform.

1.13 _____ The Tories approved of the wars during William III's reign.

1.14 _____ Jonathan Swift wrote to further the Tory cause.

1.15 _____ The Hanovers were a family of kings who were from Hanover, a small kingdom that later became part of Germany.

## THE 1750s AND AFTERWARDS

The 1750s began a period of rapid changes brought on by industrialization, shifting social classes, and continuing expansion of the British Empire. One such series of changes has sometimes been called the "agricultural revolution," although that title is probably an overstatement. It was caused by landowners who were still suffering financially from the civil war. They decided to reorganize their land and buy more land to make their farming more efficient. They then enclosed the land for their own use, a move given the title of "Enclosure Acts," and consequently prevented small farmers and squatters from using the land that had once supported them. These landowners began to develop better farming methods, such as the rotation of crops and the draining of marshes, and invented improved farm machinery, but in so doing **displaced** many of the rural poor.

Along with farming improvements in the early eighteenth century came improved spinning and mining methods. Finally, by the 1750s, spinning and weaving machinery powered by steam began what is known as the Industrial Revolution. Inventions developed rapidly to produce goods more quickly and in greater volumes.

Some of those rural poor who had been driven from their land began to cluster in newly industrialized areas to find employment. Their living conditions eventually became so intolerable that Parliament later enacted reform bills to feed and educate these groups. The Anglican Church further eroded as some members realized how the church's complicated structure prevented it from reaching the masses of poor people. The Anglican clergyman John Wesley's realization of their needs finally resulted in the Methodist break from the Church of England.

Growing industries at home and trade to other parts of the expanding British Empire produced higher-level jobs and a growing middle class. Old, established families were losing money and power, while families with unrecognized reputations began to acquire the wealth necessary to have political power. As money became more important, a classical university education became less important. Education was thinly spread at lower levels to produce a wider, but less educated, reading public, and **periodicals**, which could be read quickly and easily, were becoming more popular.

Meanwhile, England became more committed to commercial and political expansion. With the Peace of Paris at the end of the Seven Years' War in 1763, England gained the two subcontinents of Canada and India. It had given much money to protect the Americans from the French and to promote western expansion in America. The British were truly unable to understand why the Americans seemed unwilling to aid the British taxpayers. With all this show of military power came terrible costs in bloodshed and moral corruption, with emphasis on material gain and national superiority. Yet these evils were ignored by many. Only responsible thinkers such as Swift, Pope, Johnson, and Goldsmith warned of social and moral decay.

**Answer** *true* **or** *false*.

1.16 _____ The "agricultural revolution" was the enclosing of land to produce smaller estates and smaller profits.

1.17 _____ The Industrial Revolution began in the 1750s with inventions such as spinning and weaving machinery driven by steam.

1.18 _____ The masses of poor people displaced by the enclosing of land moved to poverty camps along the English coast.

1.19 _____ The Anglican clergyman whose concern for the poor eventually resulted in the Methodist denominations' break from the Church of England was Jonathan Swift.

1.20 _____ One of the lands England gained by the Peace of Paris was India.

# AUTHORS' LIVES
### (use with Events Chart)

| JOHN MILTON | JOHN BUNYAN | JONATHAN SWIFT | OLIVER GOLDSMITH |
|---|---|---|---|
| **1600** | | | |
| 1608 - Born, son of Puritan lawyer | 1628 - Born, son of artisan | | |
| 1629 - Wrote "On the Morning of Christ's Nativity" | | | |
| 1631 - Wrote *L'Allegro* and *IL Penseroso* | | | |
| 1637 - Death of mother and Edward King, wrote *Lycidas* | 1644-47 - Drafted into Parliamentary army; after war, studies Bible | | |
| 1638-39 - Travels in Italy, meets Galileo | | | |
| 1649 - Publishes two essays endorsing execution of kings, appointed Latin secretary in Cromwell's government | | | |
| **1650** | | | |
| 1652 - Wife dies becomes totally blind | 1653 - Began preaching in Baptist Churches | | |
| 1658 - second wife dies | 1660 72 - Jailed for preaching | 1667 - Born in Dublin of English parents | |
| 1660 - Arrested, fined, imprisoned for role in Cromwell's government | 1665 - Published *The Holy City* | | |
| 1667 - Published *Paradise Lost* | 1666 - Published *Grace Abounding to the Chief of Sinners* | | |
| 1671 - Published *Paradise Regained*, *Samson Agonistes* | 1675 - Jailed again, writes *Pilgrim's Progress* | | |
| 1674 - Died | 1680 - Wrote *The Life and Death of Mr. Badman* | | |
| | 1684 - Wrote Part II of *Pilgrim's Progress* | 1694 - Returned to Ireland, ordained | |
| | 1688 - Died | 1696 Wrote *A Tale of a Tub* | |
| | | 1697 Wrote *The Battle of the Books* | |

**1700**

| 1710 - | Becomes Tory, attacks Whigs in *The Examiner*, which he edited, wrote political pamphlets |
| 1713 - | Became Dean of St. Patricks. Dublin |
| 1724 - | Published the Drapier's Letters |
| 1726 - | Published Gulliver's Travels |
| 1745 - | Died |

| 1730? - | Born in Ireland |

**1750**

| 1759 - | Wrote for various periodicals, including *The Bee* |
| 1760-62 - | Published *Citizen of the World* |
| 1764 - | Published *The Traveler* |
| 1766 - | Published *The Vicar of Wakefield* |
| 1768 - | *The Good Natured Man* |
| 1770 - | Published *The Deserted Village* |
| 1771 - | Wrote She Stoops to Conquer |
| 1774 - | Died |

Chart 3

## THE REACTIONS OF WRITERS

Chart 3 illustrates that the literature of these centuries was politically conscious; major writers were deeply committed to making their readers understand the significance of current events. The two Puritans, John Milton and John Bunyan, had been active in the Commonwealth. Although forced into retirement during Charles II's reign, they reacted by emphasizing in their great works the importance of man's understanding of and devotion to God. Milton's epic poem *Paradise Lost* and Bunyan's allegory *Pilgrim's Progress* do not deal directly with political **themes**, but they emphasize faith and salvation in troubled times. They contrast with the literature written to entertain Charles II's court, literature that shows a renewed influence from France: witty and sparkling satire, carefully structured drama, and themes sometimes lacking moral values.

Writers who lived in political, economic, and social disorder were concerned with imposing order and organization on their writing. The period from 1660 to 1700 is sometimes called the Neoclassical period because writers, especially poets, used their knowledge of Greek and Latin literature to perfect literary forms. One such perfected form is the heroic couplet, which you will examine later. Most important, writers were concerned with placing man in an orderly world in which he knew his position and observed the rest of the world with educated but restrained criticism.

Writers, especially from 1688 to 1745 (sometimes called the period of Common Sense), felt a public responsibility to evaluate the quality of life, just as their classical models had. Along with this critical responsibility, they stressed the importance of a reasonable, logical approach. Realism was important in describing man's actions and his social position. Finally, a controlled approach to religion was important. They distrusted emotional shows of faith and revelations from God that would not stem from intellectual examination. They believed God works in rational ways and must be observed by the intellect. These four characteristics all appear in the works of Alexander Pope and Jonathan Swift, both of whom used satire as a weapon against, and as instruction for, the newly educated masses.

Writers from 1745 to the end of the century became more **sentimental** and even more moral. Their literature is sometimes called the Literature of **Sensibility**. These writers wrote lyrical emotional works with emphasis on the common man or on times in the distant past. They were interested in supernatural elements (usually to instruct and prepare the soul for death), and in the beauties of God in nature. They often probed the effects of melancholy.

Finally, writers found new ways to reach the public. They wrote moral or satiric essays in periodicals, such as *The Tatler* (1709), *Spectator* (1711), and *The Gentleman's Magazine* (1731). They also developed a new literary form, the novel, describing middle class people dealing with middle class problems. At that time a novel was mainly a fictitious narrative, a story having no factual basis, with a closely knit plot of epic scope and a unity of theme. John Bunyan and Daniel Defoe, the author of *Robinson Crusoe*, pioneered realistic detail and lengthened narratives. Samuel Richardson (1689–1761), Henry Fielding (1707–1754), Tobias Smollet (1721–1771), and Laurence Sterne (1713–1768) are the important novelists of the period. Their novels are still delightful to read and have influenced countless novelists since then, including Charles Dickens.

**Answer these questions.**

1.21    What are some of the characteristics of the Literature of Common Sense? _____

_____

_____

1.22    What are some of the characteristics of the Literature of Sensibility? _____

_____

_____

1.23    What are some of the characteristics of a novel? _____

_____

_____

_____

Review the material in this section in preparation for the Self Test. The Self Test will check your mastery of this particular section. The items missed on this Self Test will indicate specific areas where restudy is needed for mastery.

## SELF TEST 1

**Write the letter of the correct answer on the line** (each answer, 2 points).

1.01    The Cavaliers fought on the side of _____ in the civil war of 1642–45.

   a. the Roundheads
   b. Oliver Cromwell
   c. Charles I
   d. the Puritans

1.02    Why was there no king from 1649 to 1660? _____

   a. James I was imprisoned
   b. Charles I was executed and Parliament took control.
   c. Charles II was hidden in France by the Jacobites.
   d. James II was driven out of the country.

1.03    What one man was most powerful from 1649 to 1658? _____

   a. Oliver Cromwell
   b. Titus Oates
   c. James I
   d. Charles I

1.04    _____ was restored to the throne in 1660.

   a. Charles I
   b. Charles II
   c. James II
   d. James, the Pretender

1.05    What did the Test Act of 1672 require? _____

   a. that all government officers take communion according to the form of the Church of England
   b. that all government officers make a passing score on a standardized history test
   c. that all Puritans vow to stay in England
   d. that all Catholics vow to leave England

1.06    What was the "Popish Plot"? ____

    a.  Titus Oates' first novel

    b.  a plot to assassinate the Pope

    c.  a plot to execute Charles I

    d.  an imaginary plot in which Catholics were supposed to have planned the death of Charles II and other government officers

1.07    What was the Gunpowder Plot? ____

    a.  In 1605 France had sold gunpowder to Puritans.

    b.  In 1605 Catholic-inspired Guy Fawkes had planned to blow up the king and Parliament.

    c.  In 1605 John Dean had sold gunpowder to the pope.

    d.  In 1609 Puritan-inspired Richard Cromwell had planned to blow up the king.

1.08    Why did many English fear the Jacobites? ____

    a.  Jacob Oates had tried to blow up the Parliament.

    b.  James I had a strong army.

    c.  James II was rightful heir, but he was a Puritan.

    d.  James II was rightful heir, but he was a Catholic.

1.09    Why is the Anglican clergyman John Wesley important? ____

    a.  He invented machinery to drain the marshes.

    b.  He owned the first factory in Liverpool.

    c.  He originated the Methodist break from the Church of England.

    d.  He negotiated the Peace of Paris.

1.010   What are some characteristics of the court literature of Charles II's reign? ____

    a.  religious themes, loosely constructed plays

    b.  religious themes, serious poetry, carefully structured drama

    c.  French influence, witty satire, carefully structured drama

    d.  German influence, serious themes, lack of moral values

**Complete these sentences** (each answer, 3 points).

1.011   The Puritans began to rebel against their English king when a. _____ were enacted to force conformity to the Church of England, when no b. _____ was convened from 1629 to 1640, and when King c. _____ clearly showed a preference for the Catholic Church.

1.012   The Glorious Revolution of 1688 resulted when a. _____ sent seven bishops of the Church of England to the Tower. William of Orange from b. _____ , and his wife Mary were invited to take James II's place.  c. _____ was then given the power to determine the succession to the throne.

1.013   When the poor lost their jobs and homes in rural areas, they went to a. _____ _____ where they often lived in b. _____ .

1.014   Often people who had just acquired wealth were educated without a. _____ _____ and preferred short articles in b. _____ .

14

**Answer these questions** (each answer, 5 points).

1.015　Why did the Puritans not want to remain members of the Church of England?

_____

_____

_____

1.016　What political struggles existed during William's reign?_____

_____

_____

_____

1.017　What were the widespread economic effects resulting from the invention of steam-powered machinery?_____

_____

_____

_____

1.018　What four characteristics of the writers of the period of Common Sense can you name?

　　a. _____

　　b. _____

　　c. _____

　　d. _____

1.019　What are five characteristics of the Literature of Sensibility?

　　a. _____

　　b. _____

　　c. _____

　　d. _____

　　e. _____

**Answer** *true* **or** *false* (each answer, 1 point).

1.020　_____ *Commonwealth* is a term used to describe the Royalists' control of English government from 1649–1660.

1.021　_____ The English civil war was fought after the death of Oliver Cromwell.

1.022　_____ James II was executed during the Glorious Revolution.

1.023　_____ The Tories strongly supported William during his reign.

1.024　_____ The Hanover kings favored French over English

1.025　_____ England lost control of Canada at the end of the Seven Years' War.

1.026　_____ Although they lived in unsettled times, the Neoclassical writers strove to give their works order and organization.

1.027　_____ The Puritans did not approve of the close ties between church and state in England.

15

1.028 _____ The Enclosure Acts contributed toward providing opportunity for more efficient farming.

1.029 _____ The short story was a new literary form that resulted from the increasing size and power of the eighteenth-century middle class.

68 / 85

Score _____

Adult Check _____

Initial      Date

# II. PURITAN LITERATURE OF THE SEVENTEENTH CENTURY (1649–88)

Significant similarities characterize John Milton and John Bunyan. Both were Puritan writers who were imprisoned because of their support of the Commonwealth and their nonconformist activities. Both men had financial problems that made supporting their families difficult, yet both men remained strong in their beliefs. Finally, both wrote works of art that have influenced countless readers since their publication. Milton's great epic and Bunyan's great allegory continue to inspire readers long after much of the Royalist and Restoration literature is forgotten.

## SECTION OBJECTIVES

**Review these objectives.** When you have completed this section, you should be able to:

3. Outline John Milton's personal crises and their effect on the themes of his work.

4. Explain Milton's early interest in Christ's role in saving mankind in the poem "On the Morning of Christ's Nativity."

5. Define Milton's own attitude toward his poetic gift and his blindness in his sonnet "On His Blindness."

6. Identify Milton's purpose and his use of epic structure, recurring Biblical types, and imagery in Books I, VII, and XII of *Paradise Lost*.

7. Outline John Bunyan's biography and emphasize those events that shaped his great work *Pilgrim's Progress*.

8. Identify Bunyan's use of allegory, realistic human traits, and symbols in selections from *Pilgrim's Progress*.

## VOCABULARY

**Study these words** to enhance your learning success in this section.

| | | | |
|---|---|---|---|
| cleric | episode | pastoral elegy | vulnerability |
| contemplative | invocation | pilgrim | universal |
| elevated | Muse | | |

## JOHN MILTON (1608-1674)

Many critics of literature rank John Milton's greatness second only to Shakespeare's. His writing evokes images of heaven and hell; of good and evil; and of God, man, and Satan for countless readers. He explored in a number of his works the significance of Christ, His human **vulnerability** as well as His divine perfection. Milton probed the problems of Christians with a wise and serious honesty that had developed from studying literature of the past, contemporary issues, and personal trials.

**John Milton**

**His life.** Milton was born December 9, 1608, the son of a prosperous Puritan lawyer and amateur composer. From 1615 to 1625, he was educated privately at St. Paul's school. One biographer tells us that Milton was writing poetry at the age of ten. In 1629 he received his Bachelor of Arts degree from Christ's College, Cambridge. In that same year, just after his twenty-first birthday, he wrote his first great poem "On the Morning of Christ's Nativity." Two years later, in 1631, he wrote two more masterpieces, the companion poems *L'Allegro* and *Il Penseroso*, which present two contrasting ways of living: the active, social life and the **contemplative** life. In 1632 Milton received his Master of Arts degree and decided that he could not enter the Anglican ministry with a clear conscience because he felt unsuited for the ministry. In 1634 Milton's drama *Comus* was presented. Virtue is the theme of this drama. Milton emphasized that virtue is sincere only when it has been tested and found pure.

The year 1637 began a difficult period in which Milton's own faith was tested. Both his mother and his close friend since college, Edward King, died. Milton wrote the **pastoral elegy** *Lycidas* to probe the pain, injustices, and uncertainties of life. In that poem he handled a number of poetic styles, condemned insincere **clerics**, questioned his own future as well as that of the soul of his friend, and worked with many classical allusions. He concluded with lines that rejoice in the eternal life of Lycidas (representing his friend's eternal life):

> Weep no more, woeful shepherds weep no more,
> For Lycidas your sorrow is not dead,
> Sunk though he be beneath the watery floor,
> So sinks the day-star[1] in the Ocean bed,
> And yet anon[2] repairs his drooping head,
> And tricks[3] his beams, and with new-spangled Ore,
> Flames in the forehead of the morning sky:
> So Lycidas, sunk low, but mounted high,
> Through the dear might of him that walked the waves,
> Where other groves and other streams along,
> With Nectar pure his oozy locks he laves,[4]
> And hears the unexpressive[5] nuptial song,[6]
> In the best Kingdoms meek of joy and love.[7]

1. day-star: Sun
2. anon: soon
3. tricks: dresses
4. laves: bathes
5. unexpressive: inexpressible
6. song: marriage song of the Lamb (*Revelation* 19:9)

[7]Hughes, Merritt Y., ed. John Milton: *Complete Poems and Major Prose*. New York: The Odyssey Press, 1957.

Milton compared the dead Lycidas to the sun, which warms and guides eternally, and celebrates Lycidas' reunion with Christ.

In 1638 and 1639 Milton traveled and studied on the continent, mainly in Italy, and met the scientist Galileo and other scholars of the period. After meeting some of the greatest thinkers of his time, he began tutoring and writing political tracts with Parliamentarian (thus, Puritan) arguments. He then wrote several essays expressing his views on varied subjects. In 1644 he published *Of Education*, explaining the importance of a broadly based education, and *Areopagitica*, pleading for freedom of the press and of thought. He published *Eikonoklastes* and *Of the Tenure of Kings and Magistrates* in 1649, both endorsing the death of tyrants; these publications probably caused him to be noticed by Cromwell and, consequently, to be appointed Latin Secretary in Cromwell's Office of Foreign Affairs. In 1651 he published another essay, *Joannis Miltoni Angli Pro Populo Anglicano Defensio*, specifically defending Parliament and excusing the execution of King Charles I.

In 1652 he began to endure many personal problems. In that year his wife died in childbirth and he became totally blind. In 1658 his second wife died in childbirth. The 1660 restoration of Charles II caused Milton to be arrested, fined, and imprisoned for a short time. In 1661, while he was writing the great epic *Paradise Lost* (begun in 1658 and finished in 1665), he was bothered by financial troubles. In 1667 he finally published *Paradise Lost*.

In 1671 Milton published the shorter epic *Paradise Regained* and the dramatic poem *Samson Agonistes*. Both works help readers to understand Milton's personal suffering and temptations. In *Paradise Regained* Christ and Satan debate as Satan tries to tempt Jesus in the wilderness. Milton followed the Biblical account fairly closely, with the exception that Milton's Satan also offers Jesus political power and presents it very attractively. This power would have seemed especially important to the politically active Milton. In *Samson Agonistes*, the Biblical Samson, like Milton, is "blind among enemies" and prays for forgiveness because he has caused his own downfall by disobeying God. A comparison of the Old Testament story (Judges, Chapters 13-17) with Milton's drama will reveal that Milton gave his characters realistic emotions that could belong to any generation. Samson, in spite of his guilt and disobedience, retains his faith and is guided by God's will. With this guidance he achieves victory over the Philistines and, more importantly, over his own physical and moral weakness.

Milton died in 1674. His lofty themes, vivid poetry, political involvement, and personal trials have influenced countless poets in later generations.

**Write the letter of the correct answer on each line.**

2.1     Into what kind of family was Milton born? _____

    a. a poor Catholic family
    b. a wealthy Royalist family
    c. a prosperous Puritan family
    d. a poor Roundhead family

2.2     Why did Milton not become an Anglican minister? _____

    a. He did not think that he was suited for the Anglican ministry.
    b. His older brother decided to be the minister of the family.
    c. He did not have an adequate education to be a minister.
    d. The Anglicans would not permit him to be a minister.

2.3   What personal problem did Milton examine in his poem *Lycidas*? ____

   a. how to become famous
   b. how to deal with the loss of loved ones
   c. how to accept blindness
   d. how to remain strong in prison

2.4   What activities probably brought Milton to Oliver Cromwell's attention? ____

   a. He gave the Commonwealth money.
   b. He wrote pamphlets endorsing the death of tyrants.
   c. He fought bravely against the King's forces.
   d. He was the greatest scholar of his age.

2.5   What happened to Milton in 1652? ____

   a. His wife died and he became blind.
   b. He wrote *Paradise Lost*.
   c. He was imprisoned.
   d. He became a Catholic.

2.6   Why was Milton imprisoned? ____

   a. because he owed money to his father-in-law
   b. because he had been pro-Puritan in his publications and position
   c. because he had refused to write for Charles II
   d. because he had written pamphlets denying God's mercy

2.7   How could Milton's character Samson be compared to Milton himself? ____

   a. Both refused to marry.
   b. Both were practicing Christians.
   c. Both built temples for God.
   d. Both were blind.

**His ode: "On the Morning of Christ's Nativity."** This ode, a poem of some length with an elevated theme and a dignified manner, celebrates Christ's birth. Its joyous lines have been compared to organ music because the description of heavenly music (Stanzas IX–XIII)) swells jubilantly from the preceding quiet description of the dreary earth. The time sequence can prove difficult if the poem is not read carefully. The narrative moves from a present-tense account of Christ's birth, to the changes Jesus will make, back to the present-tense description.

A short summary should help you to appreciate and understand the poem as you read it. Stanzas I and II point out that Christmas day is the time to remember the true significance of Jesus' birth. Stanzas III and IV begin a poetic re-creation of Christ's birth; the poet instructs his **Muse** of poetry to present this ode (Line 24) to the newborn Saviour so that its music will be added to the Angelic Choir (Line 27). The Hymn itself begins by personifying Nature (or Earth) and by describing the preparations she made for her Maker (Line 43). Stanzas III–VIII describe the peace Christ brought to the earth. Stanzas IX–XIII describe the heavenly music heard by the shepherds. Milton heightens the effect of his description by using present tense in Stanza Xl to recreate the joyous sound for the reader.

In Stanza XIV the poet points out that if people could experience that heavenly music as it was at Christ's birth, "leprous sin" would melt away (Line 138); but, the poet laments, humanity must wait for the final judgment to purify the world (Stanzas XVI, XVII). In Stanza XVIII the poet consoles the reader by indicating that Christ's birth begins that purification.

Stanza XIX begins a lengthy account of all the false gods Jesus is replacing. Most of that account has been deleted here because it requires an understanding of classical mythology. Stanza XXVI concludes this parade of false gods. In Stanza XXVII the poet emphasizes again that Christ's birth is God's promise to save men from the ignorant worship of false gods and a weary existence on earth.

To appreciate Milton's skill, you should watch for certain poetic devices. Notice that darkness is always associated with the earth, but light is always associated with God, heaven, and Jesus. Notice too that silence or unpleasant noise is heard on the earth, but the music comes from heaven. The earth waits in ignorance, darkness, and silence until Jesus brings truth, light, and beautiful music.

### "ON THE MORNING OF CHRIST'S NATIVITY"

#### I

This is the Month, and this the happy morn
Wherein the Son of Heav'n's eternal King,
Of wedded Maid, and virgin Mother born,
Our great redemption from above did bring;
For so the holy sages[8] once did sing,                                    5
   That he our deadly forfeit[9] should release,
And with his Father work us a perpetual peace.

#### II

That glorious Form, that Light unsufferable,[10]
And that far-beaming blaze of Majesty,
Wherewith he wont[11] at Heav'n's high Council-Table               10
To sit the midst of Trinal Unity,
He laid aside; and here with us to be,
   Forsook the Courts of everlasting Day,
And chose with us a darksome House of mortal Clay.

8. sages: prophets
9. forfeit: penalty

10. unsufferable: unendurable
11. wont: accustomed

### III

Say Heav'nly Muse, shall not thy sacred vein[12]        15
Afford a present to the Infant God?
Hast thou no verse, no hymn, or solemn strain,
To welcome him to this his new abode,
Now while the Heav'n by the Sun's team untrod,
    Hath took no print of the approaching light,[13]    20
And all the spangled[14] host keep watch in squadrons bright?

### IV

See how from far upon the Eastern road
The Star-led Wizards[15] haste with odors sweet:
O run, prevent them with thy humble ode,
And lay it lowly at his blessed feet;    25
Have thou the honor first, thy Lord to greet,
    And join thy voice unto the Angel Choir,
From out his secret Altar toucht with hallow'd fire.

### THE HYMN

#### I

It was the Winter wild,
While the Heav'n-born child,    30
    All meanly wrapt in the rude manger lies;
Nature in awe to him
Had doff't[16] her gaudy trim,
    With her great Master so to sympathize:
It was no season then for her    35
To wanton with the Sun, her lusty Paramour.[17]

#### II

Only with speeches fair
She woos the gentle Air
    To hide her guilty front with innocent Snow,
And on her naked shame,    40
Pollute[18] with sinful blame,
    The Saintly Veil of Maiden white to throw,
Confounded that her Maker's eyes
Should look so near upon her foul deformities.

#### III

But he her fears to cease,    45
Sent down the meek-ey'd Peace;
    She crown'd with Olive green, came softly sliding
Down through the turning sphere,
His ready Harbinger,[19]
    With Turtle[20] wing the amorous clouds dividing,    50
And waving wide her myrtle wand,
She strikes a universal Peace through Sea and Land.

---

12  vein: line of thought, bed of useful mineral matter
13.  now . . . light: pre-dawn
14.  spangled: adorned
15.  wizards: wisemen
16  doff's: taken off

17.  It was . . . Paramour: an overcast day
18.  pollute: polluted
19.  Harbinger: forerunner
20.  Turtle: turtledove

## IV

No War, or Battle's sound
Was heard the World around:
   The idle spear and shield were high up hung; 55
The hooked[21] Chariot stood
Unstain'd with hostile blood,
   The Trumpet spake not to the armed throng,
And Kings sat still with awful[22] eye,
As it they surely knew their sovran Lord was by. 60

## V

But peaceful was the night
Wherein the Prince of light
   His reign of peace upon the earth began:
The Winds, with wonder whist,[23]
Smoothly the waters kiss't, 65
   Whispering new joys to the mild Ocean,
Who now hath quite forgot to rave,
While Birds of Calm sit brooding[24] on the charmed wave.

## VI

The stars with deep amaze[25]
Stand fixt in steadfast gaze, 70
   Bending one way their precious influence,
And will not take their flight,
For all the morning light,
   Or Lucifer[26] that often warn'd them thence;
But in their glimmering Orbs did glow, 75
Until their Lord himself bespake, and bid them go.

## VII

And though the shady gloom
Had given day her room,
   The Sun himself withheld his wonted[27] speed,
And hid his head for shame, 80
As his inferior flame,
   The new-enlight'n'd world no more should need;
He saw a greater Sun appear
Than his bright Throne, or burning Axletree[28] could bear.

## VIII

The Shepherds on the Lawn, 85
Or ere[29] the point of dawn,
   Sat simply chatting in a rustic row;
Full little thought they then,
That the mighty Pan[30]
   Was kindly come to live with them below; 90
Perhaps their loves, or else their sheep,
Was all that did their silly[31] thoughts so busy keep.

---

21. hooked: hooks projecting from wheels
22. awful: reverent
23. whist: hushed
24. brooding: covering with wings
25. amaze: amazement
26. Lucifer: Venus, or the sun

27. wonted: accustomed
28. Axletree: sun's chariot
29. ere: before
30. Pan: shepherd; here, Jesus
31. silly: innocent

## IX

When such music sweet
Their hearts and ears did greet,
   As never was by mortal finger struck,         95
Divinely-warbled voice
Answering the stringed noise,
   As all their souls in blissful rapture took:
The Air such pleasure loath[32] to lose,
With thousand echoes still prolongs each heav'nly close.[33]      100

## X

Nature that heard such sound
Beneath the hollow round
   Of Cynthia's seat, the Airy region thrilling,[34]
Now was almost won
To think her part was done,         105
   And that her reign had here its last fulfilling;
She knew such harmony alone
Could hold all Heav'n and Earth in happier union.

## XI

At last surrounds their sight
A Globe of circular light,         110
   That with long beams the shame-fac't night array'd,
The helmed Cherubim
And sworded Seraphim
   Are seen in glittering ranks with wings display'd,
Harping in loud and solemn choir,      115
With unexpressive[35] notes to Heav'n's new-born Heir.

## XII

Such Music (as 'tis said)
Before was never made,
   But when of old the sons of morning sung,
While the Creator Great         120
His constellations set,
   And the well-balanc't world on hinges hung,
And cast the dark foundations deep,
And bid the welt'ring waves their oozy channel keep.[36]

## XIII

Ring out ye Crystal spheres,      125
Once bless our human ears,
   (If ye have power to touch our senses so)
And let your silver chime
Move in melodious time;
   And let the Bass of Heav'n's deep Organ blow,      130
And with your ninefold harmony
Make up full consort[37] to th' Angelic symphony.

---

32. loath: hateful
33. close: cadence or conclusion of a strain in music
34. Beneath. . . thrilling: moon

35. unexpressive: inexpressible
36. While. . . keep: reference to God's creation of the world
37. consort: accompaniment

## XIV

For if such holy Song
Enwrap our fancy long,
   Time will run back, and fetch the age of gold,[38]      135
And speckl'd vanity
Will sicken soon and die,
   And leprous sin will melt from earthly mold,
And Hell itself will pass away,
And leave her dolorous[39] mansions to the peering day.      140

## XV

Yea, Truth and Justice then
Will down return to men,
   Orb'd in a Rainbow; and like glories wearing
Mercy will sit between,
Thron'd in Celestial sheen,      145
   With radiant feet the tissued clouds down steering,
And Heav'n as at some festival,
Will open wide the Gates of her high Palace Hall.

## XVI

But wisest Fate says no,
This must not yet be so,      150
The Babe lies yet in smiling Infancy, That on the bitter cross
Must redeem our loss;
   So both himself and us to glorify:
Yet first to those ychain'd[40] in sleep,      155
The wakeful trump[41] of doom mute; thunder through the deep.

## XVII

With such a horrid clang
As on mount Sinai rang
   While the red fire, and smold'ring clouds outbrake:
The aged Earth aghast      160
With terror of that blast,
   Shall from the surface to the center shake,
When at the world's last session,
The dreadful Judge in middle Air shall spread his throne.

## XVIII

And then at last our bliss      165
Full and perfect is,
   But now begins; for from this happy day
Th' old Dragon[42] under ground,
In straiter limits bound,
   Not half so far casts his usurped sway,      170
And wroth[43] to see his Kingdom fail,
Swinges[44] the scaly Horror of his folded tail.

---

38. age of gold: the Golden Age in Greek mythology, when men were good and immortal
39. dolorous: mournful
40. ychained: enchained
41. trump: trumpet
42. old Dragon: Satan
43. wroth: wrathful
44. Swinges: lashes

24

## XIX

The Oracles are dumb,
No voice or hideous hum
   Runs through the arched roof in words deceiving.      **175**
Apollo from his shrine
Can no more divine,[45]
   With hollow shriek the steep[46] of Delphos leaving.
No nightly trance or breathed spell,
Inspires the pale-ey'd Priest from the prophetic cell.      **180**

## XXVI

So when the Sun in bed,
Curtain'd with cloudy red,      **230**
   Pillows his chin upon an Orient wave,
The flocking shadows pale Troop to th' infernal jail;
   Each fetter'd Ghost slips to his several[47] grave,
And the yellow-skirted Fays[48]      **235**
Fly after the Night-steeds, leaving their Moon-lov'd maze.

## XXVII

But see! the Virgin blest, Hath laid her Babe to rest.
   Time is our tedious Song should here have ending;
Heav'n's youngest-teemed[49] Star      **240**
Hath fixt her polisht Car,
   Her sleeping Lord with Handmaid Lamp attending:
And all about the Courtly Stable,
Bright-harness'd Angels sit in order serviceable[50]

➡ **Write the letter of the correct answer on each line.**

2.8    What did Christ forsake and what did He choose? _____

   a. He left God's side to be alone in the wilderness.
   b. He left Mary's side to turn water into wine.
   c. He left heaven's council to live in "a darksome house of mortal clay.
   d. He left the "darksome earth" to join His Father.

2.9    How does Nature hide her "foul deformities"? _____

   a. with snow           c. with darkness
   b. with mud            d. with the sun

2.10   Why is the sun ashamed? _____

   a. His chariot is broken.        c. His light is inferior to Christ's.
   b. He has corrupted the earth.    d. He has lost his light.

2.11   Why would the Oracles' words be deceiving? _____

   a. They would encourage worship of false gods.
   b. They would predict false events.
   c. They would contradict each other.
   d. They would deceive Jesus.

---

45. divine: prophesy                48. Fays: fairies
46. steep: steep slope           49. teemed: born
47. several: respective         50. ibid.

2.12  The rhyme scheme of the first stanza of the introduction (Lines 1–7) is *a, b, a, b, b, c, c*; what is the rhyme scheme of the first stanza of the Hymn (Lines 29–36)? _____

    a. *a, b, a, b c, b d, d*

    b. *a, a, b, c, c, b, d, d*

    c. *a, a, b, b, c, c, d, d*

    d. *a, b, c, d, e, f, g, h*

2.13  Why would a poet use various rhyme schemes? _____

    a. to vary patterns

    b. to interest the reader

    c. to produce sounds which startle the reader

    d. to produce repetitious sounds which tie together thoughts and produce pleasure

**His sonnet: "On His Blindness"** Most scholars agree that this poem, one of his twenty-three sonnets, was written in 1652 when Milton became entirely blind. At that time he was only forty-three years old and was still active in the Commonwealth. The beginning of the poem expresses Milton's eagerness to serve God and his frustration that his blindness makes work difficult. His patience finally tells him that enduring God's will also serves Him. As you read the sonnet, notice that Milton has compared his poetic gift to the Biblical talents in Matthew 25:14–30. That comparison explains his choice of words: *spent*, *Talent*, and *account*.

Sonnet XIX

[On His Blindness]

When I consider how my light[51] is spent
    Ere[52] hall my days, in this dark world and wide,
    And that one Talent[53], which is death to hide,
    Lodg'd with me useless, though my Soul more bent
To serve therewith my Maker, and present
    My true account, lest he returning chide[54]
    "Doth God exact day-labor, light denied,"
    I fondly[55] ask; But patience to prevent
That murmur, soon replies, "God doth not need
    Either man's work or his own gifts; who best
    Bear his mild yoke,[56] they serve him best; his State
Is Kingly. Thousands at his bidding speed[57]
    And post o'er Land and Ocean without rest:
    They also serve who only stand and wait."[58]

---

51. light: sight, knowledge, spiritual light
52. Ere: before
53. Talent: coin
54. chide: shame
55. fondly: foolishly
56. yoke: an allusion to Matthew 11:28–30: "Come unto me, all ye that are heavy laden, and I will give you rest. Take my yoke upon you and learn of me; for I am meek and lowly in heart: and ye shall find rest unto your souls. For my yoke is easy, and my burden is light."
57. speed: hurry
58. ibid.

**Write the letter of the correct answer on each line.**

2.14 Read Jesus' account of the talents. Why does Milton say in Line 3 that his talent is "death to hide"? _____

    a. In Jesus' story the lazy servant is killed by robbers.

    b. In Jesus' story the servant who neglects his talent is sent "into outer darkness."

    c. In Jesus' story the servant who neglects his talent dies while trying to dig it up.

    d. In Jesus' story the servant who neglects his talent is afraid to hide it.

2.15 What does Milton mean in Line 7? _____

    a. "Does God want me to work in the day when I work better at night?"

    b. "Does God want me to work in the day?"

    c. "Does God demand work worthy of a day's labor when he has taken my vision (or spiritual light)?"

    d. "Does God want me to work at night?"

2.16 Line 11 alludes to Matthew 11:28–30 (see Note 6). How does this Biblical reference add meaning to the poem? _____

    a. Milton will never find rest until his sight is restored.

    b. Milton finds rest by working at night.

    c. Milton finds rest by working during the day.

    d. Milton finds rest when he realizes that he must accept God's will.

2.17 A sonnet is usually either Italian (Petrarchan) with the rhyme scheme *a, b, b, a, a, b, b, a, c, d, e, c, d, e,* or English (Shakespearean) with a rhyme scheme such as *a, b, a, b, c, d, c, d, e, f, e, f, g, g.* What type of sonnet is this poem? _____

    a. English or Shakespearean

    b. Spenserian

    c. Latin

    d. Italian or Petrarchan

**Answer these questions.**

2.18 What problem is expressed in the octave (first eight lines) of this sonnet. _____

_____

_____

2.19 How does Milton resolve that problem in the sestet (last six lines)?_____

_____

_____

      **His epic: _Paradise Lost_.** *Paradise Lost* is not only Milton's greatest work, but probably one of the greatest achievements in English literature. Written while Milton was blind, it nevertheless makes the mysteries of heaven and hell visible and vividly recreates the Creation of the earth. It examines the nature of evil by presenting Satan's revenge and man's disobedience, and emphasizes God's power to bring good from evil. It discusses man's free will to choose to disobey God and his ability to torture himself, to destroy his own life, or to use his moral strength to obey God. Most importantly, it comforts man by emphasizing Christ's mercy as well as God's justice. In Milton's own words, it "justifies the ways of God to men."

*Paradise Lost* is an epic poem. You have already learned in English LIFEPAC 1205 that an epic is a long narrative poem in an elevated style, having a central heroic figure, with episodes important to the history of a nation or race. *Paradise Lost's* hero is Adam, the father of mankind. The setting is vast indeed, covering heaven, earth, and hell. The poem includes numerous deeds of superhuman courage: the angels' deeds in the war in heaven, Christ's Creation of the earth and His submission of Himself to crucifixion, and Adam's acceptance of his future outside of Eden. All of these deeds are epic deeds. The poem has an elevated style that does not include rhyme. Finally, it contains epic characteristics or conventions. It opens by stating an epic theme, it has several **invocations** to Muses, it opens in the middle of the action, it has catalogs of warriors, and it contains many epic similes or stated comparisons.

The poem is quite long and is divided into twelve books. The following summary should help you to place the short selections you will be reading into the larger framework of the poem. Books I and II take place in hell, where Satan and his forces have just been driven by God's victorious army. After the introduction, which explains that the poem will tell of Adam's disobedience and the "one greater man," Christ, who restored mankind to God, you see the fallen Satan and his comrades. You learn that Satan's ambition and pride led him to defy God while still an angel and that he and his forces have been driven down to the Lake of Fire. Intending revenge, the devils debate on whether to fight openly or to use cunning. Satan finally volunteers to corrupt God's new creation, man. Satan begins a dangerous journey in which Sin, Death, and Chaos help him to reach the earth.

Book III takes place in Heaven. God sees Satan go to earth and tells Christ that Adam will disobey God. God emphasizes that He had to create Adam with free will so that his loyalty would be voluntary. God's justice requires that a life be sacrificed in order to save mankind, and Christ volunteers to sacrifice himself.

In Books IV and V Satan arrives on earth and jealously observes Adam and Eve. Adam asks the angel Raphael to tell him about heavenly things and is told the story of the fall of the angels. Books VI through VIII continue Raphael's story, with VII describing the creation of the earth and VIII telling of Adam and Eve's creation.

In Book IX Satan flatters Eve and finally convinces her to eat the fruit of the forbidden tree. Adam despairs when he discovers that Eve has disobeyed, but he eats the fruit so that he can share the consequences. In Book X, Adam and Eve begin to blame each other for their sin; but eventually they regret the damnation they have brought on their offspring and come to Christ for mercy. In Books XI and XII, the angel Michael comes to instruct and comfort Adam before turning him out of Eden with Eve. The angel tells Adam of the future of mankind and how Christ, whose birth has been prophesied, will come to save man from eternal death.

This huge work is unified by the use of recurring Biblical models or types. Adam, the first man, becomes a type of Christ, the God-man who brings a salvation that begins a new life for men. As Michael shows the future to Adam, he emphasizes that "one just man" prevents God from destroying mankind. Thus, Abdiel, Enoch, Noah, and Abraham become types of Christ. These good men of the Old Testament are essential in redeeming all men.

**Answer** *true* **or** *false.*

2.20 _____ Milton was blind when he wrote *Paradise Lost.*

2.21 _____ *Paradise Lost* discusses Man's inability to control his own life.

2.22 _____ In *Paradise Lost* the war in heaven, the creation of the earth, Christ's submission of Himself to crucifixion, and Adam's acceptance of his future outside of Eden are all epic deeds.

2.23 _____ *Paradise Lost's* poetry does not rhyme.

2.24 _____ A simile states directly (with the words "like" or "as") a comparison.

2.25 _____ The comparison "his face glowed like a candle in the dark" is a simile.

2.26 _____ In *Paradise Lost*, Satan is led by God's angels to corrupt Adam.

**Answer these questions.**

2.27 When was Adam willing to leave Eden? _____

_____

2.28 In what way is the "one just man" type important? _____

_____

This previous discussion of the meaning of the poem should not discourage you from discovering the beauty with which Milton formed his themes. Milton joyfully described the brilliance of heaven but is especially inspiring as he recounts the creation of the earth. Notice Milton's use of light and darkness in the first passage you read. In the second, ask yourself why Milton's description of the newly created fish and birds is so realistic.

Book 1, lines 1–10, 22–83, 105–16, 157–68, 242–55.

Of Man's First Disobedience, and the Fruit
Of that Forbidden Tree, whose mortal taste
Brought Death into the World, and all our woe,
With loss of Eden, till one greater Man
Restore us, and regain the blissful Seat,   5
Sing Heav'nly Muse, that on the secret top
Of Oreb, or of Sinai, didst inspire
That Shepherd,[59] who first taught the chosen Seed,[60]
In the Beginning how the Heav'ns and Earth
Rose out of Chaos: . . . . . . . . . . . . . . . . . . . . .  10

    What in me is dark
Illumine, what is low raise and support;
That to the heighth of this great Argument
I may assert Eternal providence,    25
And justify the ways of God to men.
  Say first, for Heav'n hides nothing from thy view
Nor the deep Tract of Hell, say first what cause
Mov'd our Grand Parents in that happy State,
Favor'd of Heav'n so highly, to fall off   30
From their Creator, and transgress his Will
For one restraint, Lords of the World besides?
Who first seduc'd them to that foul revolt?
Th' infernal Serpent; he it was, whose guile
Stirr'd up with Envy and Revenge, deceiv'd  35
The Mother of Mankind; what time his Pride
Had cast him out from Heav'n, with all his Host
Of Rebel Angels, by whose aid aspiring
To set himself in Glory above his Peers,

59. Shepherd: Moses
60. Seed: Israelites

He trusted to have equall'd the most High, 40
If he oppos'd; and with ambitious aim
Against the Throne and Monarchy of God
Rais'd impious War in Heav'n and Battle proud
With vain attempt. Him the Almighty Power
Hurl'd headlong flaming from the' Ethereal Sky 45
With hideous ruin and combustion down
To bottomless perdition,[61] there to dwell
In Adamantine[62] Chains and penal[63] Fire,
Who durst[64] defy th' Omnipotent to Arms.
Nine times the Space that measures Day and Night 50
To mortal men, he with his horrid crew
Lay vanquished, rolling in the fiery Gulf
Confounded[65] though immortal: But his doom
Reserv'd him to more wrath; for now the thought
Both of lost happiness and lasting pain 55
Torments him; round he throws his baleful[66] eyes
That witness'd huge affliction and dismay
Mixt with obdurate[67] pride and steadfast hate:
At once as far as Angels" ken[68] he views
The dismal Situation waste and wild, 60
A Dungeon horrible, on all sides round
As one great Furnace flam'd, yet from those flames
No light, but rather darkness visible
Serv'd only to discover sights of woe,
Regions of sorrow, doleful[69] shades, where peace 65
And rest can never dwell, hope never comes
That comes to all; but torture without end
Still urges, and a fiery Deluge, fed
With ever-burning Sulphur unconsum'd:
Such place Eternal Justice had prepar'd 70
For those rebellious, here their Prison ordained
In utter darkness, and their portion set
As far remov'd from God and light of Heav'n
As from the Center thrice to th' utmost Pole.
O how unlike the place from whence they fell! 75
There the companions of his fall, o'erwhelm'd
With Floods and Whirlwinds of tempestuous fire,
He soon discerns, and welt'ring[70] by his side
One next himself in power, and next in crime,
Long after known in Palestine, and nam'd 80
Beelzebub. To whom th' Arch-Enemy,
And thence in Heav'n call'd Satan, with bold words
Breaking the horrid silence thus began:

. . . . . . . . . . . . . . . . . . . . . . . . . . . . . . . . . .

61. perdition: damnation, hell
62. Adamantine: unyielding
63. penal: punishing
64. durst: dared
65. Confounded: destroyed

66. baleful: having deadly influence
67  obdurate: unyielding
68. ken: sight
69. doleful: sorrowful
70. welt'ring: writhing

What though the field be lost? 105
All is not lost; the unconquerable Will,
And study of revenge, immortal hate.
And courage never to submit or yield:
And what is else not to be overcome?
That Glory never shall his wrath or might 110
Extort[71] from me. To bow and sue for grace
With suppliant knee, and deify his power
Who from the terror of this Arm so late
Doubted[72] his Empire, that were low indeed,
That were an ignominy[73] and shame beneath 115
This downfall; . . . . . . . . . . . . . . . . . . . . . . .

Fall'n Cherub, to be weak is miserable
Doing or Suffering: but of this be sure,
To do aught[74] good never will be our task,
But ever to do ill our sole delight, 160
As being the contrary to his high will
Whom we resist. If then his Providence
Out of our evil seek to bring forth good,
Our labor must be to pervert that end,
And out of good still to find means of evil; 165
Which oft-times may succeed, so as perhaps
Shall grieve him, if I fail not, and disturb
His inmost counsels from their destin'd aim.

. . . . . . . . . . . . . . . . . . . . . . . . . . . . . . . .

Is this the Region, this the Soil, the Clime,
Said then the lost Arch-Angel, this the seat
That we must change for Heav'n, this mournful gloom
For that celestial light? Be it so, since he 245
Who now is Sovran[75] can dispose and bid
What shall be right: fardest[76] from him is best
Whom reason hath equall'd, force hath made supreme
Above his equals. Farewell happy Fields
Where Joy for ever dwells: Hail horrors, hail 250
Infernal world, and thou profoundest Hell
Receive thy new Possessor: One who brings
A mind not to be chang'd by Place or Time.
The mind is its own place, and in itself
Can make a Heav'n of Hell, a Hell of Heav'n.[77] 255

**Write the letter of the correct answer on each line.**

2.29 Eating of the forbidden fruit caused _____ .

   a. loss of sight

   b. loss of appetite

   c. loss of God

   d. loss of Eden

71. extort: to get by force
72. Doubted: feared for
73. ignominy: disgrace
74. aught: nothing but

75. Sovran: Sovereign
76. fardest: farthest
77. ibid.

2.30    The Muse that will inspire Milton also inspired ____ .

    a. Jesus to sacrifice himself
    b. Satan to betray God
    c. a shepherd to sow seed
    d. Moses to teach the creation of the earth

2.31    Milton asks to be enlightened with the Holy Spirit so that he can ____ .

    a. justify the ways of God to men
    b. write beautiful poetry
    c. regain his sight
    d. be released from prison

2.32    Why did Adam and Eve disobey God? ____ .

    a. They were tired of God.
    b. They did not know what they were doing.
    c. They were seduced by Satan.
    d. They were tricked by Michael.

2.33    What does Satan vow? ____ .

    a. to strengthen his army
    b. to make hell more cheerful
    c. to bring evil out of God's good
    d. to kill himself

2.34    Does Satan consider himself equal to God? (reread Lines 245–48) _____

2.35    Does Satan intend to reform? _____ Why or why not? _____

_____

2.36    Line 63 says that the fire of Hell has no light, but "darkness visible." This phrase seems to contradict itself. What do you think Milton means? _____

_____

_____

Book VII, lines 192–260, 387–448 (Christ's creation of the earth)

           Meanwhile the Son
On his great Expedition now appear'd,
Girt with Omnipotence, with Radiance crown'd,
Of majesty Divine, Sapience[78] and Love         195
Immense, and all his Father in him shone.
About his Chariot numberless were pour'd
Cherub and Seraph, Potentates and Thrones,
And Virtues, winged Spirits, and Chariots wing'd.
From the Armory of God, where stand of old        200
Myriads between two brazen Mountains lodg'd
Against a solemn day, harness't at hand,
Celestial Equipage; and now came forth
Spontaneous. for within them Spirit liv'd,
Attendant on their Lord: Heav'n op'n'd wide        205
Her ever-during[79] Gates, Harmonious sound
On golden Hinges moving, to let forth

78. Sapience: wisdom                  79. ever-during: enduring

The King of Glory in his powerful Word
And Spirit coming to create new Worlds.
On heav'nly ground they stood, and from the shore                   210
They view'd the vast immeasurable Abyss
Outrageous as a Sea, dark, wasteful, wild,
Up from the bottom turn'd by furious winds
And surging waves, as Mountains to assault
Heav'n's heighth, and with the Centre mix the Pole.                 215
  Silence, ye troubl'd waves, and thou Deep, peace,
Said then th' Omnific[80] Word, your discord end:
  Nor stay'd, but on the Wings of Cherubim
Uplifted, in Paternal Glory rode
Far into Chaos, and the World unborn;                               220
For Chaos heard his voice: him all his train
Follow'd in bright procession to behold
Creation, and the wonders of his might.
Then stay'd the fervid Wheels, and in his hand
He took the golden Compasses, prepar'd                              225
In God's Eternal store, to circumscribe
This Universe, and all created things:
One foot he centred, and the other turn'd
Round through the vast profundity[81] obscure,
And said, Thus far extend, thus far thy bounds,                     230
This be thy just Circumference, O World.
Thus God the Heav'n created, thus the Earth,
Matter unform'd and void: Darkness profound
Cover'd th' Abyss: but on the wat'ry calm
His brooding wings the Spirit of God outspread,                     235
And vital virtue infused, and vital warmth
Throughout the fluid Mass, but downward purg'd
The black tartareous[82] cold Infernal dregs
Adverse to life; then founded, then conglob'd[83]
Like things to like, the rest to several place                     240
Disparted,[84] and between spun out the Air,
And Earth selfbalanc't on her Centre hung.
  Let there be Light, said God, and forthwith Light
Ethereal,[85] first of things, quintessence[86] pure
Spring from the Deep, and from her Native East                     245
To journey through the airy gloom began,
Spher'd in a radiant Cloud, for yet the Sun
Was not; she in a cloudy Tabernacle
Sojourn'd the while. God saw the Light was good;
And light from darkness by the Hemisphere                          250
Divided: Light and Day, and Darkness Night
He nam'd. Thus was the first Day Ev'n and Morn:
Nor pass'd uncelebrated, nor unsung
By the Celestial Choirs, when Orient Light
Exhaling first from Darkness they beheld;                          255
Birth-day of Heav'n and Earth; with joy and shout

---

80. Omnific: all-creating
81. profundity: depths
82. tartareous: hell-like
83. conglob'd: formed in a round mass

84. Disparted: separated
85. Ethereal: heavenly, celestial
86. quintessence: the pure essence

The hollow Universal Orb they fill'd,
And touch'd their Golden Harps, and hymning prais'd
God and his works, Creator him they sung,
Both when first Ev'ning was, and when first Morn. 260

. . . . . . . . . . . . . . . . . . . . . . . . . . . . .

    And God said, let the Waters generate
Reptile[87] with Spawn[88] abundant, living Soul:[89]
And let Fowl fly above the Earth with wings
Display'd on the op'n Firmament[90] of Heav'n. 390
And God created the great Whales, and each
Soul living, each that crept, which plenteously
The waters generated by their kinds,
And every Bird of wing after his kind;
And saw that it was good, and bless'd them, saying; 395
Be fruitful, multiply, and in the Seas
And Lakes and running Streams the waters fill;
And let the Fowl be multipli'd on the Earth.
Forthwith the Sounds and Seas, each Creek and Bay
With Fry[91] innumerable swarm, and Shoals 400
Of Fish that with their Fins and shining Scales
Glide under the green Wave, in Sculls[92] that oft
Bank the mid Sea; part single or with mate
Graze the Seaweed their pasture, and through Groves
Of Coral stray, or sporting with quick glance 405
Show to the Sun their wav'd coats drops with Gold,
Or in their Pearly shells at ease, attend
Moist nutriment, or under Rocks their food
In jointed Armor watch: on smooth the Seal,
And bended Dolphins play: part huge of bulk 410
Wallowing unwieldly,[93] enormous in their Gait
Tempest the Ocean: there Leviathan[94]
Hugest of living Creatures, on the Deep
Stretcht like a Promontory[95] sleeps or swims,
And seems a moving Land, and at his Gills 415
Draws in, and at his Trunk spouts out a Sea.
Meanwhile the tepid Caves, and Fens and shores
Their Brood as numerous hatch from th' Egg that soon
Bursting with kindly[96] rupture forth disclos'd
Their callow[97] young, but feather'd soon and fledge[98] 420
They summ'd their Pens[99] and soaring th' air sublime
With clang despis'd the ground, under a cloud
In prospect; there the Eagle and the Stork
On Cliffs and Cedar tops their Eyries[100] build
Part loosely wing the Region, part more wise 425
In common, rang'd in figure wedge their way,
Intelligent of seasons, and set forth
Their Aery Caravan high over Seas

---

87. Reptile: including fish
88. Spawn: offspring
89. living Soul: life
90. Firmament: vault
91. Fry: young fish
92. Sculls: schools
93. unwieldly: heavily

94. Leviathan: large sea animal
95. Promontory: high point of land extending into the water
96. kindly: natural
97. callow: unfeathered
98. fledge: feathered
99. summ'd their Pens: developed a complete set of feathers
100. Eyries: nests

Flying, and over Lands with mutual wing
Easing their flight; so steers the prudent Crane,                              430
Her annual Voyage, borne on Winds; the Air
Floats,[101] as they pass, fann'd with unnumber'd plumes:
From Branch to Branch the smaller Birds with song
Solaced the Woods, and spread their painted wings
Till Ev'n, nor then the solemn Nightingale                                     435
Ceas'd warbling, but all night tun'd her soft lays:
Others on Silver Lakes and Rivers Bath'd
Their downy Breast; the Swan with Arched neck
Between her white wings mantling[102] proudly, Rows
Her state with Oary feet: yet oft they quit                                    440
The Dank,[103] and rising on stiff Pennons[104] tow'r
The mid Aereal Sky: Others on ground
Walk'd firm; the crested Cock whose clarion[105] sounds
The silent hours, and th' other whose gay Train
Adorns him, color'd with the florid[106] hue                                   445
Of Rainbows and Starry Eyes. The Waters thus
With Fish replenish", and the Air with Fowl,
Ev'ning and Morn solemniz'd the Fift day.[107]

**➤ Write the letter of the correct answer on each line.**

2.37   In Milton's account of the Creation, how does Christ create the circumference of the world? ____

    a. with God's compasses
    b. with a rope from God's waist
    c. with Heaven's golden chains
    d. with dust

2.38   What did the Holy Spirit do? ____

    a. The Spirit did nothing.
    b. The Spirit created man.
    c. The Spirit introduced virtue and warmth into the mass Jesus had circumscribed.
    d. The Spirit paved a road through Chaos.

2.39   What happened when light was created? ____

    a. Jesus rested.
    b. The sun and moon were created.
    c. Man was created.
    d. The angels celebrated.

2.40   What letter is alliterated or repeated in Lines 417-21? ____

    a. *b*   b. *c*   c. *f*   d. *g*

2.41   Why would a poet want to use alliteration? ____

    a. to make the words look more attractive
    b. to please by repeating sounds
    c. because he could not think of another letter
    d. because words would then be more meaningful

101. Floats: is tanned into waves
102: mantling: spreading
103: Dank: the deep
104. Pennons: wings

105. clarion: clear, sharp, shrill
106. florid: rosy, highly colored
107. ibid.

2.42  Why would alliterated *s*'s add to the description of a fire? _____

_____

2.43  How is Milton's description of birds realistic? _____

_____


Book XII, lines 552–605, 625–49 (Adam and Eve's departure from Eden)

and thus Adam last repli'd:
How soon hath thy prediction, Seer blest,
Measur'd this transient[108] World, the Race of time,
Till time stand fixt: beyond is all abyss,                                    555
Eternity, whose end no eye can reach.
Greatly instructed I shall hence depart,
Greatly in peace of thought, and have my fill
Of knowledge, what this Vessel can contain;
Beyond which was my folly to aspire.                                        560
Henceforth I learn, that to obey is best,
And love with fear the only God, to walk
As in his presence, ever to observe
His providence, and on him sole depend,
Merciful over all his works, with good                                      565
Still overcoming evil, and by small
Accomplishing great things, by things deemed[109] weak
Subverting worldly strong, and worldly wise
By simply meek; that suffering for Truth's sake
Is fortitude to highest victory,                                             570
And to the faithful Death the Gate of Life;
Taught this by his example whom I now
Acknowledge my Redeemer ever blest.
To whom thus also th' Angel last repli'd:
This having learnt, thou hast attained the sum                              575
Of wisdom; hope no higher, though all the Stars
Thou knew'st by name, and all th' ethereal Powers
All secrets of the deep, all Nature's works,
Or works of God in Heav'n, Air, Earth, or Sea,
And all the riches of this World enjoy'dst,                                  580
And all the rule, one Empire; only add
Deeds to thy knowledge answerable, add Faith,
Add Virtue, Patience, Temperance, add Love,
By name to come call'd Charity, the soul
Of all the rest: then wilt thou not be loath[110]                           585
To leave this Paradise, but shalt possess
A paradise within thee, happier far
Let us descend now therefore from this top
Of Speculation; for the hour precise
Exacts our parting hence; and see the Guards,                               590

108. transient: passinq away with time
109. deemed: believed, considered
110. loath: reluctant

36

By me encampt on yonder Hill, expect
Their motion, at whose Front a flaming Sword,
In signal of remove, waves fiercely round;
We may no longer stay: go, waken Eve;
Her also I with gentle Dreams have calm'd                    595
Portending[111] good, and all her spirits compos'd
To meek submission: thou at season fit
Let her with thee partake what thou hast heard,
Chiefly what may concern her Faith to know,
The great deliverance by her Seed to come                    600
(For by the Woman's Seed) on all Mankind,
That ye may live, which will be many days,
Both in one Faith unanimous though sad,
With cause for evils past, yet much more cheer'd
With meditation on the happy end.                            605

. . . . . . . . . . . . . . . . . . . . . . . . . . . . . . .

       now too nigh[112]                         625
Th' Arch-Angel stood, and from the other Hill
To their fixt Station, all in bright array
The Cherubim descended; on the ground
Gliding meteorous,[113] as Ev'ning Mist
Ris'n from a River o'er the marish[114] glides,              630
And gathers ground fast at the Laborer's heel
Homeward returning. High in Front advanc't,
The brandisht[115] Sword of God before them blaz'd
Fierce as a Comet; which with torrid heat,
And vapor as the Libyan Air adust,[116]                      635
Began to parch that temperate Clime; whereat
In either hand the hast'ning Angel caught
Our ling'ring Parents, and to th' Eastern Gate
Led them direct, and down the Cliff as fast
To the subjected[117] Plain; then disappear'd.              640
They looking back, all th' Eastern side beheld
Of Paradise, so late their happy seat,
Wav'd over by that flaming Brand, the Gate
With dreadful Faces throng'd and fiery Arms:
Some natural tears they dropp'd, but wip'd them soon;       645
The World was all before them, where to choose
Their place of rest, and Providence their guide:
They hand in hand with wand'ring steps and slow,
Through Eden took their solitary way.[118]

---

111.  portending: foreshadowing
112.  nigh: near
113.  meteorous: like a cloud
114.  marish: marsh

115.  brandisht: swinging
116.  adust: burnt
117.  subjected: lying beneath
118.  ibid.

2.44    Christ and Adam have manhood in common. Yet, Adam and Eve also resemble Satan: Adam had disobeyed God, Eve had been ambitious enough to challenge God's knowledge, and both had blamed each other rather than themselves for their disobedience. What words in Line 561 show that Adam has learned what Satan never could? _____

    a.  to forget revenge
    b.  to forget ambition
    c.  to obey God
    d.  to stay away from women

2.45    How does the "one just man" theme tie in with Lines 565–70? _____

    a.  One man is not strong enough to subvert the worldly strong.
    b.  One good man, though weak, can accomplish great things.
    c.  A man should be worldly wise but never weak.
    d.  One good man should not be made to suffer for Truth's sake.

2.46    How do these lines agree with Milton's sonnet "On His Blindness"? _____

    a.  Both poems say evil is too powerful.
    b.  Both poems say strength is the best talent.
    c.  Both poems say God expects weakness.
    d.  Both poems say that small things may accomplish God's will.

**Answer these questions.**

2.47    Compare Lines 586–87 with those spoken by Satan in Book I: "The mind is its own place, and in itself/ Can make a Heav'n of Hell, a Hell of Heav'n" _____

_____

_____

_____

2.48    Michael speaks in Lines 600–602 of " The great deliverance by her Seed to come/ (For by the Woman's Seed) on all Mankind,/ That ye may live." What is he talking about? _____

2.49    Lines 627–32 contain a simile. How do you know it is a simile? What does it mean?_____

_____

_____

_____

**Complete this activity.**

2.50    On a separate sheet of paper write a one-page essay in which you explain why you think Adam's paradise is or is not lost. Give the essay to your teacher for evaluation.

Adult Check    _____
                        Initial      Date

## JOHN BUNYAN (1628-1688)

John Bunyan was both a writer and a preacher. As a writer he used a style noted for its simplicity and force. As a preacher he was dedicated enough to persist in his vocation even though he suffered penalties for doing so.

John Bunyan

**His life.** John Bunyan was born in 1628, the son of a tinker (a mender of household utensils). He later became a tinker himself. At sixteen he was drafted into the Parliamentary army and served from November 1644 to June 1647. Afterwards he began to study the Bible, which later became the textbook for the power, simplicity, narrative skill, and rhythm of his own writing.

In 1653 he joined a Baptist Church in Bedford and began preaching his own sermons. He published a tract against jeering Quakers, entitled *Some Gospel Truths Opened*, in 1656. At the Restoration of Charles II, Bunyan was found guilty of disobeying the Conventicle Act, forbidding nonconformists to preach or publish, and was imprisoned for twelve years, until 1672. Thus, most of his writing was done in prison. He was given opportunities to be released from jail, but lost them because he refused to promise to discontinue preaching. While in prison, he frequently preached to his fellow prisoners.

In 1666 he wrote *Grace Abounding to the Chief of Sinners*, telling of his own intense religious struggles. *The Holy City* (written in 1665) was influenced by Revelation and anticipated his description of heaven in *Pilgrim's Progress*. In 1672 he wrote another account of his own faith, *A Confession of My Faith and a Reason of My Practice*.

After he was released from prison, he was elected pastor of his own church; nonconformists were then permitted to preach. His sermons were popular and he attracted large crowds even when he traveled in London. After three years, however, preaching was again banned; and he was imprisoned for six more months during which time he wrote the first part of *Pilgrim's Progress,* which was published later in 1678. He published *The Life and Death of Mr. Badman* in 1680, an allegory about a fashionable man who becomes a hypocritical Christian. Several critics find this work anticipates Defoe in its use of realistic details. *The Holy War*, published in 1682, tells of Bunyan's military experiences. It is a social allegory about Mansoul, a town needing salvation. Much detail is given to the politics of leaders. Bunyan described the evils of his own times, especially the mistreatment of nonconformists. In 1684 the second part of *Pilgrim's Progress* appeared, describing the fate of Christian's wife and family. Bunyan died in 1688.

**Answer** *true* or *false*.

2.51 _____ John Bunyan was drafted into the Royalist army.

2.52 _____ Bunyan learned his writing style at Oxford University.

2.53 _____ In 1660 nonconformist preaching was against the law.

2.54 _____ Bunyan was in prison for only about six months.

2.55 _____ Bunyan's writing is admired for its simplicity, realistic detail, and narrative skill.

2.56 _____ Bunyan's study of the Bible, his sermons, and his military experiences did not influence his work.

**His allegory: *Pilgrim's Progress*.** Bunyan's greatest allegory has become a popular classic in English literature; it was widely read in Puritan New England as well as in England. It is in the form of an allegorical journey from the City of Destruction to the Celestial City, and it explains the doctrine of salvation in detail. It has interested readers as well as taught them because the symbolic landscapes and characters are also realistically described. Christian himself is both a **universal pilgrim** and a poor, nervous man from Bedfordshire. Because the reader sympathizes with Christian, he is eager to go with him, to solve each segment of the allegory. The allegory is also skillfully told; suspense continues from **episode** to episode. Bunyan's style is simple, direct, and lacks difficult classical references. In addition, Bunyan included social satire in his section "Vanity Fair." The poor pilgrims chained by the merchants closely parallel the Puritans imprisoned after the Restoration.

You should understand what an allegory is and why it is used. An allegory is a form of comparison lengthened into a story. Objects, persons, and actions in this story represent general concepts or moral qualities that lie outside the story and are parts of the doctrine or theme being presented. The characters in an allegory are usually personifications of abstract qualities such as Hope and Faith (remember the personification of Nature in Milton's poem "On the Morning of Christ's Nativity;" in that poem the earth takes on the personality of a woman). The action and setting of an allegory are representative of relationships among these abstractions. Thus, the reader is interested in the literal story and characters presented, but is also aware of the ideas behind the story. In *Pilgrim's Progress*, the character, Christian, makes an actual journey. He flees from the City of Destruction; struggles through such places as the Slough of Despond, the Valley of the Shadow of Death, and Vanity Fair; and finally arrives at the Celestial City. Christian meets actual characters named Evangelist, Faithful, Hopeful, and Giant Despair. This story, however, represents the efforts of one man to save his soul by triumphing over inner obstacles to his faith. Bunyan used the allegory to make his doctrine of salvation interesting and persuasive.

Bunyan's symbols, things or actions that represent something else, are logical and are realistically described. Bunyan used character and place names that quickly explain what they represent. Thus Christian meets a devil who tries to discourage him in a very logical place, the Valley of Humiliation. Giant Despair, who tries to convince Christian to commit suicide, lives at Doubting Castle. Bunyan's symbolic use of objects is usually obvious; for example, Christian, who has become mentally burdened by worries about his destruction, is symbolically weighted down by a burden on his back. Yet these symbolic characters, places, and objects are not entirely one-dimensional; they are described with realistic details that are interesting in themselves. Christian is so weak and nervous that he allows his family to belittle him and honestly tells Evangelist that he does not see the wicket-gate in the distance and is not even sure he sees the light. Giant Despair loses his temper easily and is nagged by a meddling wife named Diffidence.

Bunyan understood emotions and thoughts so well that Christian's journey is complex enough for even the most thoughtful Christian. Christian is made to doubt his own worth, to torture himself with guilt, to suffer so much that he considers suicide, and to fear death even as he sees the Celestial City. Bunyan did not try to teach by oversimplifying.

Finally, he knew how to tell a good story. He dropped clues and repeated events with interesting variety to build suspense. As Christian asks himself once again "What shall I do?" or waits for Giant Despair to come back once more, the reader is so interested that he truly wants to see what happens. Understandably, the popularity of *Pilgrim's Progress* has been second only to that of the Bible.

# LANGUAGE ARTS

## ARTS

1 2 0 7

## LIFEPAC TEST

68 / 85

**Name**_____

**Date** _____

**Score** _____

# ENGLISH 1207: LIFEPAC TEST

**Answer** *true* **or** *false* (each answer, 1 point).

1. _____ Periodicals and the novel became more popular as the more powerful middle class began to read.

2. _____ Milton was imprisoned because of his previous position in the Commonwealth.

3. _____ The Puritans felt that the Anglican Church was incorruptible.

4. _____ James I was restored to the throne in 1660.

5. _____ When public land was enclosed for private estates, most of the rural poor were allowed to stay.

6. _____ John Bunyan studied the Bible carefully after the civil war.

7. _____ Oliver Goldsmith wrote a biography of Samuel Johnson.

8. _____ In The Deserted Village Goldsmith praises the sentimental village preacher.

9. _____ Oliver Goldsmith believed that one can never be too rich.

10. _____ Samuel Johnson wrote periodical essays in only one newspaper.

**Match these items** (each answer, 2 points).

11. _____ repetition of initial consonants      a. heroic couplet

12. _____ giving the appearance of saying one thing while meaning something else      b. allegory

     c. satire

13. _____ a comparison using "like" or "as"      d. sentimental

14. _____ consists of two rhyming lines of verse with five iambic feet      e. alliteration

15. _____ giving something human characteristics      f. simile

16. _____ a story in which things represent parts of a doctrine or theme      g. irony

17. _____ a poem with fourteen lines, either Italian or English      h. personification

18. _____ ridiculing something in order to correct behavior      i. sonnet

19. _____ Swift's, Johnson's, Goldsmith's political party      j. Tory

20. _____ tone in The Deserted Village      k. Whig

**Write the letter of the correct answer** (each answer, 2 points).

21. How are Bunyan's characters in Pilgrim's Progress more than just symbols? _____
     a. They have names such as Christian, Hope, and Ignorance.
     b. They do not belong in the story.
     c. They represent abstract steps in the process of salvation.
     d. They are individuals described with realistic details.

22. What one result did the Commonwealth and the Industrial Revolution have? _____
     a. a strong monarchy
     b. a strong middle class
     c. a strong lower class
     d. a strong aristocracy

23. For which cause did Swift *not* write? _____
   a. the Tory government
   b. the devaluation of Irish coins
   c. the Whig wars under William III
   d. the starvation in Ireland

24. Which of the following items does not appear in *Gulliver's Travels* to satirize **English society?** _____
   a. the Howhows and their dogs
   b. the Lilliputians and their Emperor
   c. the king of the Brobdingnagians
   d. the Laputans and their flappers

25. Which of the following items is *not* an example of poetic diction? _____
   a. labouring swain
   b. swimming fish
   c. sheltered cot
   d. mirthful band

26. Samuel Johnson believed that literature should appeal mainly to _____ .
   a. the scholar, to please him
   b. the common man, to teach him
   c. the common man, to teach and please him
   d. the king and the Parliament

27. In *The Deserted Village* the poet emphasizes the loss of the village by saying that _____ .
   a. much money was lost when the villagers left
   b. most of the villagers died of starvation
   c. no one will miss the place
   d. he himself had planned to retire there

28. What was *not* happening in the second half of the eighteenth century? _____
   a. decreased trade with other countries
   b. a growing British Empire
   c. the Industrial Revolution
   d. the "agricultural revolution"

29. Samuel Johnson did *not* publish _____ .
   a. *The Vicar of Wakefield*
   b. *A Dictionary of the English Language*
   c. *The Lives of the English Poets*
   d. *Rasselas*

30. Oliver Goldsmith _____ .
   a. was a famous lawyer
   b. was a wealthy doctor and clergyman
   c. was an Anglican clergyman who wrote for the Tories
   d. was a financially poor periodical essayist, novelist, and dramatist

**Complete these sentences** (each answer, 3 points).

31.   In *The Deserted Village* the villagers are driven from their homes because the _____ _____ Acts have enabled a wealthy landowner to buy the public property.

32.   In that same poem (31) the poet says that the villagers will either go to America or to crowded, corrupted _____ .

33.   In the book _____ , the king of Brobdingnag observes that most men are not morally suitable for their jobs.

34.   Goldsmith wrote a _____ entitled *The Vicar of Wakefield*, about a parson's family.

35.   At the end of *The Deserted Village*, _____ leaves with the rural virtues and the displaced villagers because people left in England are too corrupted by wealth to appreciate art.

**Answer these questions** (each answer, 5 points).

36.   In *Paradise Lost* why is Adam finally willing to leave Eden?_____
_____
_____

37.   In "On the Morning of Christ's Nativity," what did Christ forsake and what did He choose?
_____
_____

38.   In "On His Blindness," what does Milton regret? _____
_____
_____

39.   What is *Pilgrim's Progress* about? _____
_____
_____

**Write the letter of the correct answer on each line.**

2.57  An allegory _____

    a. is something that stands for something else
    b. is a story in which things, people, and actions represent parts of a doctrine or theme
    c. is a short comparison
    d. is giving human characteristics to something not human

2.58  *Pilgrim's Progress* is about _____

    a. a man who brings his family to Vanity Fair
    b. a man who drowns in the River of Death
    c. a man who fights in the civil war
    d. a man who saves his soul

2.59  The character Christian _____

    a. is very active and does not think about his problems
    b. is a puppet for Bunyan's teachings
    c. has a personality of his own
    d. is always sure about himself

**Answer** *true* **or** *false*.

2.60  _____ *Pilgrim's Progress* does not make sense unless you "read in" the deeper meaning.

2.61  _____ Christian's journey is an example for any man who needs spiritual help.

**"Do You See Yonder Shining Light?"**

41

As I walked through the wilderness of this world, l lighted on a certain place where was a Den, and I laid me down in that place to sleep; and, as I slept, I dreamed a dream. I dreamed, and behold I saw a man clothed with rags, standing in a certain place, with his face from his own house, a book in his hand, and a great burden upon his back (Isaiah, 64:6; Luke, 14:33; Psalms, 38:4; Habakkuk, 2:2; Acts, 16:31). I looked and saw him open the book and read therein; and, as he read, he wept, and trembled; and not being able longer to contain, he brake out with a lamentable cry, saying, "What shall I do?" (Acts, 2:37).

In this plight, therefore, he went home and refrained himself as long as he could, that his wife and children should not perceive his distress; but he could not be silent long, because that his trouble increased. Wherefore at length he brake his mind to his wife and children; and thus he began to talk to them. O my dear wife, said he, and you the children of my bowels, I, your dear friend, am in myself undone by reason of a burden that lieth hard upon me; moreover, I am for certain informed that this our city will be burned with fire from heaven, in which fearful overthrow both myself, with thee, my wife, and you my sweet babes, shall miserably come to ruin, except (the which yet I see not) some way of escape can be found, whereby we may be delivered. At this his relations were sore amazed; not for that they believed that what he had said to them was true, but because they thought that some frenzy distemper had got into his head; therefore, it drawing towards night, and they hoping that sleep might settle his brains, with all haste they got him to bed. But the night was as troublesome to him as the day; wherefore, instead of sleeping, he spent it in sighs and tears. So, when the morning was come, they would know how he did. He told them, Worse and worse: he also set to talking to them again: but they began to be hardened. They also thought to drive away his distemper by harsh and surly carriages[119] to him; sometimes they would deride,[120] sometimes they would chide,[121] and sometimes they would quite neglect him. Wherefore he began to retire himself to his chamber, to pray for and pity them, and also to condole[122] his own misery; he would also walk solitarily in the fields, sometimes reading, and sometimes praying: and thus for some days he spent his time.

Now, I saw, upon a time, when he was walking in the fields, that he was, as he was wont,[123] reading in his book, and greatly distressed in his mind; and as he read, he burst out, as he had done before, crying, "What shall I do to be saved?"

I saw also that he looked this way and that way, as if he would run; yet he stood still, because, as I perceived, he could not tell which way to go. I looked then, and saw a man named Evangelist[124] coming to him, who asked, Wherefore dost thou cry? (Job, 33:23)

He answered, Sir, I perceive by the book in my hand that I am condemned to die, and after that to come to judgment (Hebrews, 9:27), and I find that I am not willing to do the first (Job, 16:21), nor able to do the second (Ezekiel, 22:14).

Then said Evangelist, Why not willing to die, since this life is attended with so many evils? The man answered, Because I fear that this burden that is upon my back will sink me lower than the grave, and I shall fall into Tophet[125] (Isaiah, 30:33). And, sir, if I be not fit to go to prison, I am not fit to go to judgment, and from thence to execution; and the thoughts of these things make me cry.

Then said Evangelist, If this be thy condition why standest thou still? He answered, Because I know not whither to go. Then he gave him a parchment roll, and there was written within, "Flee from the wrath to come" (Matthew, 3:7).

The man therefore read it, and looking upon Evangelist very carefully, said, Whither must I fly? Then said Evangelist, pointing with his finger over a very wide field, Do you see yonder wicket-gate? (Matthew, 7:13, 14). The man said, No. Then said the other, Do you see yonder shining light? (Psalms, 119:105; 2 Peter, 1:19). He said, l think I do. Then said Evangelist, Keep that light in your eye, and go up directly thereto: so shalt thou see the gate; at which when thou knockest it shall be told thee what thou shalt do. So I saw in my dream that the man began to run. Now, he had not run far from his own door, but his wife and children perceiving it, began to cry after him to return; but the man put his fingers in his ears, and ran on, crying, Life! Life! eternal life! (Luke, 14:26.) So he looked not behind him, but fled towards the middle of the plain (Genesis, 19:17).

119. **carriages:** outward behavior
120. **deride:** ridicule, make fun of
121. **chide:** scold
122. **condole:** sympathize with

123. **wont:** accustomed to do
124. **Evangelist:** preacher
125. **Trophet:** hell

**Write the letter of the correct answer on each line.**

2.62 What does the burden on Christian's back symbolize? _____

    a. his sin and guilt
    b. his family's disease
    c. his wound caused by a fire
    d. his money

2.63 How does Christian's family respond to his worry? _____

    a. They cry with him.
    b. They ask for proof of his news.
    c. They belittle and neglect him.
    d. They put him in an institution.

2.64 Why is Evangelist the appropriate character to show Christian the way? _____

    a. An evangelist preaches the Gospel.
    b. Evangelist was the only man Christian knew.
    c. Evangelist had a map of heaven.
    d. Christian would not listen to anyone else.

2.65 What does Christian fear? _____

    a. becoming blind
    b. meeting Satan
    c. his journey
    d. dying and being judged

**Answer this question.**

2.66 What details make this story more realistic? _____

_____

_____

### [The Vision of Vanity Fair]

Then I saw in my dream, that when they were got out of the wilderness, they presently saw a town before them, and the name of that town is Vanity and at the town there is a fair kept; called Vanity Fair: it is kept all the year long; it beareth the name of Vanity Fair, because the town where it is kept is lighter[126] than vanity; and also because all that is there sold, or that cometh thither, is vanity. As is the saying of the wise, "all that cometh is vanity" (Ecclesiastes, 1:2, 14; 2:11, 17; 11:8; Isaiah, 51:29).

This fair is no new-erected business, but a thing of ancient standing; I will show you the original[127] of it.

Almost five thousand years agone, there were pilgrims walking to the Celestial City, as these two honest persons[128] are: and Beelzebub Apollyon, and Legion,[129] with their companions perceiving by the path that the pilgrims made, that their way to the city lay through this town of Vanity, they contrived here to set up a fair, a fair wherein should be sold all sorts of vanity, and that it should last all the year long: therefore at this fair are all such merchandise sold, as houses, lands, trades, places, honors, preferments, titles, countries, kingdoms, lusts, pleasures, and delights of all sorts, as whores, bawds, wives, husbands, children, masters, servants, lives, blood, bodies, souls, silver, gold, pearls, precious stones, and what not.

126. lighter: more unimportant
127. original: source or history

128. two honest persons: Christian and Hope
129. Beelzebub Apollyon, and Legion: devils

And, moreover, at this fair there is at all times to be seen juggling, cheats, games, plays, fools, apes,[130] knaves, and rogues, and that of every kind.

Here are to be seen, too, and that for nothing, thefts, murders, adulteries, false swearers, and that of a blood-red color.

And as in other fairs of less moment,[131] there are the several rows and streets, under their proper names, where such and such wares are vended; so here likewise you have the proper places, rows, street (viz. countries and kingdoms), where the wares of this fair are soonest to be found. Here is the Britain Row, the French Row, the Italian Row, the Spanish Row, the German Row, where several sorts of vanities are to be sold. But, as in other fairs, some one commodity is as the chief of all the fair, so the ware of Rome[132] and her merchandise is greatly promoted in this fair; only our English nation, with some others, have taken a dislike threat.

Now, as I said, the way to the Celestial City lies just through this town where this lusty fair is kept; and he that will go to the City, and yet not go through this town, must needs "go out of the world" (1 Corinthians, 5:10). The Prince of princes himself, when here, went through this town to his own country, and that upon a fair day too; yea, and as I think, it was Beelzebub the chief lord of this fair, that invited him to buy of his vanities; yea, would have made him lord of the fair, would he but have done him reverence as he went through the town. (Matthew, 4:8; Luke, 4:5-7.) Yea, because he was such a person of honor, Beelzebub had him from street to street, and showed him all the kingdoms of the world in a little time, that he might, if possible, allure the Blessed One to cheapen[133] and buy some of his vanities; but he had no mind to the merchandise, and therefore left the town, without laying out so much as one farthing upon these vanities. This fair, therefore, is an ancient thing, of long standing, and a very great fair. Now these pilgrims, as I said, must needs go through this fair. Well, so they did: but, behold, even as they entered into the fair, all the people in the fair were moved, and the town itself as it were in a hubbub about them; and that for several reasons: for—

First, the pilgrims were clothed with such kind of raiment as was diverse from the raiment of any that traded in that fair. The people, therefore, of the fair, made a great gazing upon them: some said they were fools, some they were bedlams,[134] and some they are outlandish men. (1 Corinthians, 2:7, 8.)

Secondly, And as they wondered at their apparel, so they did likewise at their speech; for few could understand what they said; they naturally spoke the language of Canaan[135] but they that kept the fair were the men of this world: so that, from one end of the fair to the other, they seemed barbarians each to the other.

Thirdly, But that which did not a little amuse the merchandisers was, that these pilgrims set very light by all their wares, they cared not so much as to look upon them; and if they called upon them to buy, they would put their fingers in their ears, and cry, "Turn away mine eyes from beholding vanity," and look upwards, signifying that their trade and traffic was in heaven. (Psalms, 119:37; Philippians, 3:19, 20.)

One chanced mockingly, beholding the carriage of the men, to say unto them, What will ye buy? But they, looking gravely upon him, answered, "We buy the truth" (Proverbs, 23:23). At that there was an occasion taken to despise the men the more; some mocking, some taunting, some speaking reproachfully, and some calling upon others to smite them. At last things came to a hubbub and great stir in the fair, insomuch that all order was confounded. Now was word presently brought to the great one of the fair, who quickly came down, and deputed[136] some of his most trusty friends to take these men into examination, about whom the fair was almost overturned. So the men were brought to examination; and they that sat upon them, asked them whence they came, whither they went, and what they did there, in such an unusual garb? The men told them that they were pilgrims and strangers in the world, and that they were going to their own country, which was the heavenly Jerusalem (Hebrews, 11:13-16); and that they had given no occasion to the men of the town, nor yet to the merchandisers, thus to abuse them, and to let them in their journey, except it was for that, when one asked them what they would buy, they said they would buy the truth. But they that were appointed to examine them did not

---

130. apes: probably people who mimic
131. moment: importance
132. ware of Rome: Roman Catholic ritual
133. cheapen: ask the price of

134. bedlams: madmen
135. Canaan: district in Palestine
136. deputed: delegated

believe them to be any other than bedlams and mad, or else such as came to put all things into a confusion in the fair. Therefore they took them and beat them, and besmeared them with dirt, and then put them into the cage, that they might be made a spectacle to all the men of the fair.

> Behold Vanity Fair! the Pilgrims there
> Are chained and stand beside:
> Even so it was our Lord passed here,
> And on Mount Calvary died.

**Write the letter of the correct answer on each line.**

2.67    How would you describe Vanity Fair? _____
    a. It is a place unlike the society we know.
    b. It is a place of busy pride and showy worthlessness.
    c. It is a part of the Celestial City.
    d. It is a new place.

2.68    Describe the goods at Vanity Fair. _____
    a. They are not worth much money.
    b. They are what most people consider valuable and desirable.
    c. They have nothing to do with everyday life.
    d. They would not interest most people.

2.69    Why did Bunyan entitle the streets Britain Row, French Row, and so on? _____
    a. to give the reader familiar names
    b. to confuse the reader
    c. to make it clear that Vanity Fair is the world
    d. to confuse Christian

2.70    Who is the Prince of Princes mentioned? _____
    a. Christian           c. Hope
    b. Satan             d. Christ

2.71    Who did Bunyan probably have specifically in mind when he described the pilgrims who resisted worldly temptations and were chained because of their beliefs? _____
    a. Catholics          c. Anglicans
    b. nonconformists    d. Jews

Review the material in this section in preparation for the Self Test. The Self Test will check your mastery of this particular section. The items missed on this Self Test will indicate specific areas where restudy is needed for mastery.

**Answer** *true* **or** *false* (each answer, 1 point).

2.01 _____ James II was restored to the throne in 1660.

2.02 _____ When the poor lost their jobs and homes in rural areas, they went to newly industrialized areas where they often lived in slums.

2.03 _____ The Puritans felt that the Anglican Church was corrupted by unnecessary ritual, by organization that was no longer able to reach each member, and by control of a corrupt government and monarchy.

2.04 _____ Periodicals and the novel became popular as the more powerful **middle class** began to read.

2.05 _____ Milton was born into a prosperous Puritan family.

2.06 _____ Milton lost his sight in childhood.

2 07 _____ Milton was imprisoned because he had refused to write for Charles II.

2.08 _____ Milton wrote pamphlets endorsing the death of kings.

2.09 _____ John Bunyan studied the Bible carefully after the civil war.

2.010 _____ John Bunyan was imprisoned because he was an Anglican minister.

**Match these items** (each answer, 2 points).

2.011 _____ 1649–60 government without a king

2.012 _____ 1688 invitation to William and Mary

2.013 _____ 1750s inventions with steam power

2.014 _____ a fourteen-line poem, Italian or English

2.015 _____ a comparison using "like" or "as"

2.016 _____ a long narrative poem in an elevated style with a hero and episodes important to a nation or race

2.017 _____ the repetition of initial consonants

2.018 _____ a story in which things represent parts of a doctrine or theme

2.019 _____ something that stands for something else

2.020 _____ things given human characteristics

a. epic

b. simile

c. the Restoration

d. alliteration

e. allegory

f. the Commonwealth

g. the Industrial Revolution

h. personification

i. symbol

j. sonnet

k. the Glorious Revolution

**Write the letter of the correct answer on each line** (each answer, 2 points).

2.021 The rhyme scheme of the following lines is: _____

High diddle diddle,
The Cat and the Fiddle,
The Cow jumped over the moon.
The little Dog laughed
To see such craft,
And the Dish ran away with the Spoon.

a. *a, b, a, b, c, c*

b. *a, a, b, b, c, c*

c. *a, a, b, c, c, b*

d. *a, a, b, c, c, d*

2.022 In "On the Morning of Christ's Nativity," Christ's birth does not cause _____ .

    a. momentary peace on earth       c. a speech by Satan

    b. heavenly music                d. classical oracles to be silenced

2.023 In "On His Blindness," Milton regrets _____ .

    a. his blindness               c. that God is so unfair

    b. that his blindness restricts his work    d. that he is in prison

2.024 In "On His Blindness," Milton finally assures himself that _____ .

    a. he must accept God's will, that he must "stand and wait."

    b. he will regain his sight

    c. he wilt get all his work done

    d. he will forget his mother's death

2.025 In *Paradise Lost*, Adam, the father of mankind, is _____ .

    a. taken to heaven to meet God       c. lost in Chaos

    b. a comic character             d. an epic hero

2.026 Adam, Noah, and Christ are all examples of _____ .

    a. men with flaws             c. men who resist Satan

    b. the type "one just man"        d. men who sacrifice themselves

2.027 Milton's account of the Creation of the earth shows that _____ .

    a. the Biblical account is wrong

    b. God, Jesus, and the Holy Spirit created the world with great love

    c. even Christ became tired of such a job

    d. the world was created by accident

2.028 Before Adam and Eve are led out of Eden, Michael shows Adam a vision _____ .

    a. in which Adam sees the Creation of the world

    b. in which Adam sees Satan destroyed by flood waters

    c. in which Adam sees the future and Christ's redemption

    d. in which Adam sees the creation of Eve

2.029 Bunyan's writing was formed by his experience _____ .

    a. studying and teaching at Oxford

    b. studying the Bible, preaching sermons, and serving in the army

    c. studying Latin and translating it

    d. nursing his mother back to health

2.030 *Pilgrim's Progress* is about _____ .

    a. a man who fights in the civil war

    b. a man who brings his family to Vanity Fair

    c. a man who learns the way of salvation

    d. a man who drowns in the River of Death

**Complete these sentences** (each answer, 3 points).

2.031 A poet uses _____ at the end of lines to tie together thoughts and to produce pleasure with the repetitious sounds.

2.032 An Italian _____ poses a problem in the first eight lines, the octave, and resolves the problem in the last six lines, the sestet.

2.033 In "On the Morning of Christ's Nativity," Nature's covering herself with snow is an example of _____ .

2.034 Unlike Satan, who will always defy God, Adam learns _____ to God.

2.035 The line, "The blazing brightness of her beauties became," contains examples of _____ .

**Answer these questions** (each numbered answer, 5 points).

2.036 What are five of the things in Milton's personal life that influenced his writing?

    a. _____

    b. _____

    c. _____

    d. _____

    e. _____

2.037 What is the main idea of "On the Morning of Christ's Nativity"? _____

_____

_____

_____

2.038 In the sonnet "On His Blindness," what does Milton mean in the last line: "They also serve who only stand and wait"? _____

_____

_____

2.039 How are Abdiel, Enoch, Noah, Abraham, and Christ all of the same type in *Paradise Lost*?

_____

_____

_____

_____

2.040 In *Paradise Lost*, what does Michael mean when he tells Adam this?

        Add Virtue, Patience, Temperance, add Love,
        By name to come call'd Charity, the soul
        Of all the rest: then wilt thou not be loath
        To leave this Paradise, but shalt possess
        A paradise within thee, happier far.

_____

_____

_____

2.041 How are Bunyan's characters in *Pilgrim's Progress* more than just symbols?

_____

_____

76
95

Score _____

Adult Check _____

                                Initial      Date

# III. SATIRE FROM THE LITERATURE
## OF COMMON SENSE (1688-1745)

Several writers observing the many changes in the period from the Glorious Revolution to the 1750s felt that only common sense would solve accompanying political, economic, social, and cultural problems. They stressed the importance of recognizing and criticizing current problems, using a reasonable and logical approach to deal with the problems, and describing the problems with realistic details. They were able to be critical, reasonable, and realistic by using satire, a literary manner that belittles a subject to produce wit and humor. Of the writers who used satire, Alexander Pope and Jonathan Swift are noted for their sincere alarm over changes they considered harmful and are enjoyed for their entertaining and polished writing.

## SECTION OBJECTIVES

**Review these objectives.** When you have completed this section, you should be able to:

9. Outline the major events in the life of Alexander Pope.
10. Define the methods and forms Pope used in his satire.
11. Outline Jonathan Swift's biography, with emphasis on the political and religious activities that most influenced his satire.
12. Explain Swift's satiric purpose in short passages from *Gulliver's Travels*.

## VOCABULARY

Study these words to enhance your learning success in this section.

| | | |
|---|---|---|
| barb | digression | intimate |
| beau | exclusive | misanthrope |
| burlesque | inflated | rational |

## ALEXANDER POPE (1688-1744)

A poet and satirist, Alexander Pope became a literary giant of his age. Indeed, he could not be ignored or taken lightly. His harsh attacks on his contemporaries earned him the title of the "Wicked Wasp of Twickenham" (Twickenham is the name of the village in which he resided).

**His life**. Born in 1688, Alexander Pope had to overcome two serious personal problems. He was born a Roman Catholic during a time when Catholics were discriminated against; and at twelve he was afflicted with tuberculosis of the spine, which left him physically unattractive and weak. He nevertheless became perhaps the greatest poet between Milton and Wordsworth and a close friend of an author you will study in more detail, Jonathan Swift. His famous poems, including *Essay on Criticism*, *The Rape of the Lock*, *Windsor Forest*, *Eloisa to Abelard*, *The Dunciad*, and *Imitations of Horace*, made him one of the

**Alexander Pope**

first professional poets; that is, a poet who makes his living by writing poetry. His classical learning brought additional income. He published translations both of the *Illiad* and the *Odyssey*. He died a famous and respected poet in 1744.

**His satire**. You should be familiar with Pope's important contributions to literature and to the society of his time. Both he and Jonathan Swift were members of a small writers' organization called the Scriblerus Club, which was formed specifically to satirize the foolish and vain studies and hobbies of their age. The members of this club wrote poetry, essays, long fictional works, and plays to belittle worthless studies and practices. Their works entertain because they make their subjects ridiculous, but they also teach indirectly because they **intimate** that other practices are better than the ones being discouraged through ridicule.

This ridiculing effect is achieved by several methods. An author may magnify and exaggerate the corruption of the object being satirized. He may also position the satirized object next to something very undignified so that there is "guilt by association"; a person compared to a dog is made as foolish as a dog. Another widely used method is irony, the appearance of saying or being one thing while making it clear to the audience that something different is meant. Thus, although the simple-minded Gulliver in Swift's *Gulliver's Travels* admires what he sees, the reader understands that he is *not* supposed to admire the same thing. Oftentimes a praise-blame inversion is used: The author seems to praise something, but the reader realizes that he is actually condemning it.

Alexander Pope used all these methods skillfully in his two most famous satires *The Rape of the Lock* and his longer mock epic *The Dunciad*. In *The Rape of the Lock*, Pope satirized polite society by representing a disagreement at a card game among young ladies and their **beaux** as an epic battle. The disagreement (over one young man's cutting a lock of his lady's hair) was made to look insignificant and silly when given such **inflated** comparisons. Pope made excellent use of irony. *The Dunciad* records all the epic games and activities of writers and publishers as they make their epic journey through London. Its satire is bitter and angry; it concludes with Dulness sitting on her throne in darkness. Pope, as all the writers of the *Scriblerus Club*, was alarmed that culture as he knew it was disappearing and that society would be controlled by those who were only half-educated.

Pope used an already perfected poetic form, the heroic couplet, for most of his satires; but he made that form so flexible that no other poet has matched Pope's skill. The heroic couplet consists of two rhyming lines of verse with five iambic feet per line; an iambic foot, or unit of rhythm, consists of an unstressed syllable (marked ˘) followed by a stressed syllable (marked ´).

**Examples:**

| *1st foot* | *2nd foot* | *3rd foot* | *4th foot* | *5th foot* |
|---|---|---|---|---|
| ˘ ´ | ˘ ´ | ˘ ´ | ˘ ´ | ˘ ´ |
| Avoid | extremes; | and shun | the fault | of such, |
| ˘ ´ | ˘ ´ | ˘ ´ | ˘ ´ | ˘ ´ |
| Who still | are pleased | too lit | tle or | too much. |

The preceding lines should help you to understand five-beat lines. These two-line units conclude with the second line completing the thought, forming a closed couplet. Because the heroic couplet is so tightly constructed, it is an ideal vehicle for **barbs** of satire. Pope could use the heroic couplet to tell stories, to present realistic conversation, or to give memorable statements about his own philosophy. His satiric genius in the following lines from *The Dunciad* combined the heroic couplet form, a parody (or humorous imitation) on Milton's account of Creation, and a comparison of poorly written verse to maggots:

> Here she [Dulness] beholds the Chaos dark and deep,
> Where nameless Somethings in their causes sleep,
> Till genial Jacob, or a warm Third day,
> Call forth each mass, a Poem, or a Play:
> How hints, like spawn, scarce quick in embryo lie,
> How newborn nonsense first is taught to cry,
> Maggots half formed in rhyme exactly meet,
> And learn to crawl upon poetic feet.
>
> (*The Dunciad*, Bk.I. 11. 55–62)

These lines illustrate Pope's tightly constructed poetry, entertainingly witty lines, and biting criticism of the rapid changes taking place at every level of society.

**Answer *true* or false.**

3.1 _____ Alexander Pope was born a Roman Catholic but had many friends because of his physical attractiveness.

3.2 _____ Pope, along with Jonathan Swift, was a member of the Scriblerus Club, a group of writers satirizing society.

3.3 _____ A satirist may make a subject ridiculous by comparing it to something undignified.

3.4 _____ A satirist may also use irony, which gives the appearance of saying one thing while meaning something else.

**Write the letter of the correct answer.**

3.5 A heroic couplet consists of _____ .

   a. two rhyming lines of verse with four iambic feet
   b. two unrhyming lines of verse with five iambic feet
   c. two rhyming lines of verse with five iambic feet
   d. two rhyming lines of verse with five trochaic feet

3.6 Pope used the heroic couplet _____ .

   a. infrequently, only in letters
   b. infrequently, usually to tell stories
   c. frequently, to narrate, to present realistic conversation, to give memorable statements, or to give short satiric barbs
   d. frequently, to write plays and essays

### JONATHAN SWIFT (1667–1745)

Jonathan Swift was a poet, satirist, political writer, and clergyman. Although he called himself a **misanthrope**, he always wrote to help improve humanity.

**Jonathan Swift**

**His life.** Jonathan Swift was born in 1667 in Dublin, Ireland. Many of his religious and political activities and the resulting writing originated from his early Irish background. In 1694 he was ordained in the Anglican church. He began his satiric writing early while a secretary to Sir William Temple in England. He wrote *A Tale of a Tub* (published in 1704) to satirize corruptions in religion and learning. The tale describes the adventures of three brothers who care for their coats in different ways. Peter, representing the Roman Catholics, adorns his coat until it cannot be recognized; Jack, representing dissenters, tears his coat by taking off Peter's decorations too quickly and carelessly; and Martyn, representing the Anglicans, saves his coat by making changes slowly and preserves it according to the instructions given in his father's will. The tale also contains many **digressions** satirizing critics, both ancient and modern learning, and even madness. In 1697 he wrote *The Battle of the Books* (published in 1704), a satire in which the Ancients (books written by Homer, Pindar, Euclid, Aristotle, and Plato) win a battle begun by the Moderns (books by Milton, Dryden, and others). Swift emphasized the importance of classical learning when he compared the Moderns to a spider that spins webs from its own filth and the Ancients to a bee that gets its honey by tasting from several flowers already blossoming.

51

Then Swift became more involved in Irish issues. From 1707 to 1709, he sought to do away with a tax on Irish clerical incomes. Later in 1724 he wrote the first four *Drapier's Letters*, which protest the use of low value, overabundant copper coins produced outside of Ireland without Irish permission. The letters, written to encourage the boycott of the new coins, raised the attention both of the English and the Irish. The English considered the writer of the letters dangerous and offered a reward for the arrest of the Drapier (Swift did not use his own name); Swift's printer was actually arrested. The Irish, on the other hand, considered Swift a great patriot. His writing was so persuasive that the order for the coins was canceled. In 1729 Swift again worked for Irish causes by publishing *A Modest Proposal*, a satire emphasizing the brutal indifference the English demonstrated toward the starving Irish. He accused the British Parliament of cruelty and satirized social mathematicians or economists of the period who saw people as commodities rather than suffering individuals.

As he was involved with Irish problems, he was also active in English political circles. From 1710 to 1714, he was in London in the midst of an **exclusive** group of Tories. He was, perhaps, the greatest propagandist for the Tory government. He believed that enemies of the Tories were also enemies of culture and morality, and thus turned his satire against them. He hated the unreasonable and cruel qualities of men when they joined into groups to gain their own ends, but he believed that individual men could be responsible for their own behavior. He, therefore, sought to persuade men to be responsible and reasonable.

Swift suffered disappointments because of his intense involvement in political and religious issues. Even though he had wanted a bishop's office in England, he was made Dean of St. Patrick's Cathedral in Dublin; Queen Anne disapproved of some of the lower forms of satire in *A Tale of a Tub* and would never consent to granting him a higher office. The following year, in 1714, Queen Anne died and Swift's former political activities with the Tories alienated him from the new Whig government.

In 1726 he stayed in England with Alexander Pope and published *Gulliver's Travels*. He published several *Miscellanies* with Pope in 1727 and 1728. In 1738 he was suffering intense pain from Méniére's syndrome, causing physical imbalance, nausea, deafness, and eventually, madness. He died in 1748 and was buried in St. Patrick's Cathedral in Dublin. His sense of critical responsibility, his wit, his use of realistic detail, and his easily read style have entertained countless readers.

**Write the letter of the correct answer.**

3.7 Swift's satire that tells of three brothers' coats is _____ .

　　a. *Gulliver's Travels*
　　b. *A Tale of a Tub*
　　c. *The Dunciad*
　　d. *Paradise Lost*

3.8 Swift was _____ .

　　a. a Puritan preacher
　　b. a professional poet
　　c. a member of Parliament
　　d. an ordained Anglican clergyman

3.9 Swift showed his Irish patriotism by writing about _____ .

　　a. starvation and the devaluation of coins in Ireland
　　b. Irish members of Parliament
　　c. the superiority of Irish Whigs
　　d. poor farming techniques and alcoholism in Ireland

3.10 Swift wrote for _____ .

    a. the Whigs

    b. the Tories

    c. the Scots

    d. the Welsh

3.11 Swift approved of powerful political groups _____ .

    a. only if individual members made a financial gain

    b. only if they were approved by Queen Anne

    c. only if they had Christian goals

    d. only if individual members were reasonable and responsible for their own behavior

**His satire: *Gulliver's Travels*.** Swift's best-known work is often introduced to children because of its realistic and exciting adventures. It is, however, a satire operating at several levels that teaches older readers as well as entertains them; it is a political satire, a **burlesque** of voyage books, and a satire on the abuses of reason and vanity. Its story is told by a fictitious sailor named Gulliver.

In the first book, Captain Gulliver is shipwrecked on the coast of Lilliput where people are only six inches tall. In this book Gulliver is shocked by these short, but politically and morally corrupt people who often represent immoral English politicians. Gulliver feels superior morally as well as physically.

In the second part, Gulliver is in Brobdingnag, and is dwarfed by giants sixty feet tall. Here, he learns that he, too, is corrupt as he compares his former way of life to that of these practical, benevolent giants. Swift used the satiric method of associating moral corruption with physical corruption by having Gulliver examine the giants' human characteristics; Gulliver sees enlarged corruption to remind him that the human condition is also coarse and repulsive.

In the third book, Gulliver himself is less important than the travels he describes. He visits several countries where the inhabitants (scholars, scientists, philosophers, inventors, professors) appear ridiculous in their over-reliance on reason as opposed to common sense.

In the fourth book, the naive Gulliver becomes increasingly disenchanted with his own kind. He begins to worship **rational**, unemotional horse-beings, the Houyhnhnms. He compares himself to the human-like but beastly Yahoos, who are held in subjection by the Houyhnhnms, and learns to hate men for not being horses. Here, Swift's satire is double-edged; the cold Houyhnhnms are imperfect, just as the Yahoos are. Gulliver is disabled by his self-hate; he becomes too critical and isolated to love even his own family.

The short passages you will read should be fitted into this larger framework. Gulliver learns to be more critical, but eventually he becomes so aware of imperfections that he is unable to feel a natural human warmth toward his own kind. Swift's use of irony allows the reader to see that Gulliver's final hate has driven him mad. Swift's style is clear and easy to read, and his use of concrete details is convincing. He frequently used irony and comparisons with undignified subjects to satirize both the practices and the political and cultural figures of the period.

**Write the letter of the correct answer.**

3.12  Which people in *Gulliver's Travels* most often represent English political figures? _____

    a.  the Brobdingnagians        c.  the Lilliputians

    b.  the Houyhnhnms         d.  the Welsh

3.13  What effect does seeing the Brobdingnagians' enlarged human features have on Gulliver? _____

    a.  He is reminded of man's corruption.        c.  He fears the size of their feet.

    b.  He admires their large eyes.        d.  He thinks the Brobdingnagians look like horses

3.14  The Houyhnhnms cause Gulliver to _____

    a.  love himself        c.  improve himself

    b.  love his family        d.  hate himself

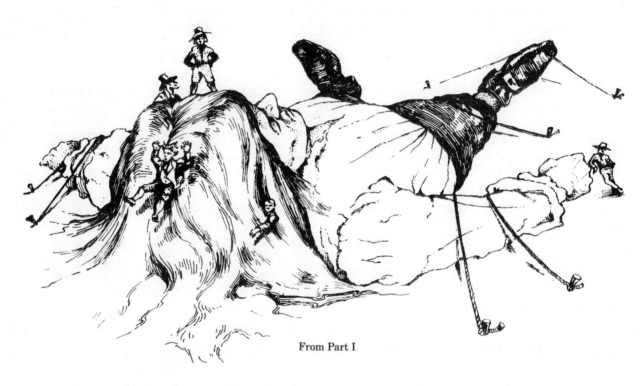

From Part I

We therefore trusted ourselves to the mercy of the waves, and in about half an hour the boat was overset by a sudden flurry from the north. What became of my companions in the boat, as well as of those who escaped on the rock, or were left in the vessel, I cannot tell; but conclude they were all lost. For my own part, I swam as fortune directed me, and was pushed forward by the wind and tide. I often let my legs drop, and could feel no bottom: but when I was almost gone and able to struggle no longer, I found myself within my depth; and by this time the storm was much abated. The declivity[1] was so small, that I walked near a mile before I got to the shore, which I conjectured was about eight o'clock in the evening. I then advanced forward near half a mile, but could not discover any sign of houses or inhabitants; at least I was in so weak a condition, that I did not observe them. I was extremely tired, and with that, and the heat of the weather, and about half a pint of brandy that I drank as I left the ship, I found myself much inclined to sleep. I lay down on the grass, which was very short and soft, where I slept sounder than ever I remember to have done in my life, and, as I reckoned, above nine hours; for when I awaked, it was just daylight. I attempted to rise, but was not able to suit for as I happened to lie on my back, I found my arms and legs were strongly fastened on each side of the ground; and my hair, which was long and thick, tied down in the same manner. I likewise felt several slen-

1. declivity: descending slope

der ligatures[2] across my body, from my armpits to my thighs. I could only look upwards, the sun began to grow hot, and the light offended my eyes. I heard a confused noise about me, but, in the posture I lay, could see nothing except the sky. In a little time I felt something alive moving on my left leg, which advancing gently forward over my breast, came almost up to my chin; when, bending my eyes downwards as much as I could, I perceived it to be a human creature not six inches high, with a bow and arrow in his hands, and a quiver at his back. In the mean time, I felt at least forty more of the same kind (as I conjectured) following the first. I was in the utmost astonishment, and roared so loud, that they all ran back in a fright; and some them, as I was afterwards told, were hurt with the falls they got by leaping from my sides upon the ground....

My gentleness and good behaviour had gained so far on the Emperor and his court, and indeed upon the army and people in general, that I began to conceive hopes of getting my liberty in a short time. I took all possible methods to cultivate this favourable disposition. The natives came by degrees to be less apprehensive of any danger from me. I would sometimes lie down, and let five or six of them dance on my hand. And at last the boys and girls would venture to come and play at hide and seek in my hair. I had now made a good progress in understanding and speaking their language. The Emperor had a mind one day to entertain me with several of the country shows, wherein they exceed all nations I have known, both for dexterity and magnificence. I was diverted with none so much as that of the ropedancers, performed upon a slender white thread, extended about two foot, and twelve inches from the ground. Upon which I shall desire liberty, with the reader's patience, to enlarge a little.

This diversion is only practiced by those persons who are candidates for great employments, and high favour, at court. They are trained in this art from their youth, and are not always of noble birth, or liberal education. When a great office is vacant either by death or disgrace (which often happens) five or six of those candidates petition the Emperor to entertain his Majesty and the court with a dance on the rope, and whoever jumps the highest without falling, succeeds in the office. Very often the chief ministers themselves are commanded to show their skill, and to convince the Emperor that they have not lost their faculty. Flimnap, the Treasurer, is allowed to cut a caper on the strait rope, at least an inch higher than any other lord in the whole empire, I have seen him do the summerset several times together upon a trencher[3] fixed on the rope, which is no thicker than a common packthread in England.

**Answer these questions.**

3.15 The first excerpt describes Gulliver's escape from his sinking ship and the Lilliputians' discovery of him. What types of details make this account convincing? _____

_____

_____

_____

_____

3.16 In the second excerpt, Gulliver observes the Emperor of the Lilliputians (who represents King George I) and those of his court who seek his favor. Flimnap, the Treasurer, represents the famous Whig statesman, Sir Robert Walpole, who was head of the government from 1715 to 1717 and from 1721 to 1742. Both individuals are satirized. Yet Swift also satirized types of people in his account of rope dancing. What type of person do you think is satirized? _____

_____

_____

2. ligatures: things used in typing or binding together
3. trencher: wooden platter for serving food

**3.17** Review the methods of satire discussed in the selection on Alexander Pope's satire and name the one that Swift used in the second excerpt. _____

_____

_____

### From Part II

It is the custom that every Wednesday (which, as I have before observed, was their Sabbath) the King and Queen, with the royal issue of both sexes, dine together in the apartment of his Majesty, to whom I was now become a favourite; and at these times my little chair and table were placed at his left hand before one of the salt-cellars. This prince took a pleasure in conversing with me, enquiring into the manners, religion, laws, government, and learning of Europe, wherein I gave him the best account I was able. His apprehension was so clear, and his judgment so exact, that he made very wise reflections and observations upon all I said. But I confess, that after I had been a little too copious[4] in talking of my own beloved country, of our trade, and wars by sea and land, of our schisms[5] in religion, and parties in the state, the prejudices of his education prevailed so far, that he could not forbear taking me up in his right hand, and stroking me gently with the other, after an hearty fit of laughing, asked me whether I were a Whig or a Tory. Then turning to his first minister, who waited behind him with a white staff, near as tall as the main-mast of the *Royal Sovereign*, he observed how contemptible[6] a thing was human grandeur,[7] which could be mimicked by such diminutive[8] insects as I: And yet, said he, I dare engage, those creatures have their titles and distinctions of honour, they contrive little nests and burrows, that they call houses and cities; they make a figure in dress and equipage;[9] they love, they fight, they dispute, they cheat, they betray.... You have clearly proved that ignorance, idleness and vice are the proper ingredients for qualifying a legislator. That laws are best explained, interpreted, and applied by those whose interest and abilities lie in perverting, confounding, and eluding them. I observe among you some lines of an institution, which in its original might have been tolerable, but these half erased, and the rest wholly blurred and blotted by corruptions. It doth not appear from all you have said, how any one perfection is required towards the procurement[10] of any one station among you, much less that men are ennobled on account of their virtue, that priests are advanced for their piety or learning, soldiers for their conduct or valour, judges for their integrity, senators for the love of their country, or counsellors for their wisdom. As for yourself, continued the King, who have spent the greatest part of your life in travelling, I am well disposed to hope you may hitherto have escaped many vices of your country. But, by what I have gathered from your own relation, and the answers I have with much pains wringed and extorted from you, I cannot but conclude the bulk of your natives to be the most pernicious[11] race of little odious vermin that nature ever suffered to crawl upon the surface of the earth.

4. **copious:** rich, plentiful
5. **schisms:** formal separation from a church or religious body
6. **contemptible:** worthy of contempt or scorn
7. **grandeur:** first in importance, dignified, great
8. **diminutive** tiny
9. **equipage:** an outfit, a set of articles, a carriage
10. **procurement:** an obtainment, an achievement by getting possession of something
11. **Pernicious:** deadly, wicked

**Answer these questions.**

3.18  In this part Gulliver discusses his country with the sixty-foot king of Brobdingnag. The king listens to Gulliver's description and then delivers his own judgment. Do you think that we are meant to respect the king's judgment? _____

_____

3.19  The king compares humans to something undignified. What comparison does he make?

_____

_____

3.20  In this section, what details indicate that Swift intended his own society to be satirized?

_____

_____

3.21  Does the king think that men in Swift's England are qualified for their positions?

_____

_____

## From Part III

I walked a while among the rocks; the sky was perfectly clear, and the sun so hot, that I was forced to turn my face from it: when all on a sudden it became obscured, as I thought, in a manner very different from what happens by the interposition of a cloud. I turned back, and perceived a vast opaque body between me and the sun, moving forwards towards the island: it seemed to be about two miles high, and hid the sun six or seven minutes, but I did not observe the air to be much colder, or the sky more darkened, than if I had stood under the shade of a mountain.... I took out my pocket-perspective,[12] and could plainly discover numbers of people moving up and down the sides of it, which appeared to be sloping, but what those people were doing I was not able to distinguish.... But at the same time the reader can hardly conceive my astonishment, to behold an island in the air, inhabited by men, who were able (as it should seem) to raise, or sink, or put it into a progressive motion, as they pleased.... They made signs for me to come down from the rock, and go towards the shore, which I accordingly did; and the flying island being raised to a convenient height, the verge directly over me, a chain was let down from the lowest gallery, with a seat fastened to the bottom, to which I fixed my self, and was drawn up by pulleys.

At my alighting I was surrounded by a crowd of people, but those who stood nearest seemed to be of better quality.... Their heads were all reclined either to the right, or the left; one of their eyes turned inward, and the other directly up to the zenith. Their outward garments were adorned with the figures of suns, moons, and stars, interwoven with those of fiddles, flutes, harps, trumpets, guitars, harpsichords, and many more instruments of music, unknown to us in Europe.[13] I observed here and there many in the habits of servants, with a blown bladder[14] fastened like a flail[15] to the end of a short stick, which they carried in their hands. In each bladder was a small quantity of dried pease[16] or little pebbles (as I was afterwards informed). With these bladders they now and then flapped the mouths and ears of those who stood near them, of which practice I could not then conceive the meaning; it seems, the minds of these people are so taken up with intense speculations, that they neither can speak, nor attend to the discourses of others, without being roused by some external taction[17] upon the organs of speech and hearing; for which reason those persons who are able to afford it always keep a flapper (the original is *cli-*

---

12.  perspective: spyglass, telescope
13.  sun, ...Europe: satire of George I's court in which much attention was paid to abstract science and the theory of music

14.  bladder: a sac resembling a bladder
15.  flail: a short, swinging stick attached to a wooden handle
16.  pease: peas
17.  taction: contact, touch

*menole)* in their family, as one of their domestics, nor ever walk abroad or make visits without him. And the business of this officer is, when two or more persons are in company, gently to strike with his bladder the mouth of him who is to speak, and the right ear of him or them to whom the speaker addresseth himself. This flapper is likewise employed diligently to attend his master in his walks, and upon occasion to give him a soft flap on his eyes, because he is always so wrapped up in cogitation,[18] that he is in manifest danger of falling down every precipice, and bouncing his head against every post, and in the streets, of jostling others or being jostled himself into the kennel[19] it was necessary to give the reader this information, without which he would be at the same loss with me, to understand the proceedings of these people, as they conducted me up the stairs, to the top of the island, and from thence to the royal palace. While we were ascending, they forgot several times what they were about, and left me to my self, till their memories were again roused by their flappers; for they appeared altogether unmoved by the sight of my foreign habit and countenance, and by the shouts of the vulgar,[20] whose thoughts and minds were more disengaged.

**Answer these questions.**

3.22 What does Gulliver see as he is walking in the midst of rocks? _____

_____

3.23 What could this country (Laputa) that Gulliver discovers symbolize? _____

_____

_____

_____

3.24 Why do the Laputans' attentions have to be gotten by using a flapper? _____

_____

_____

_____

### From Part IV

When I thought of my family, my friends, my countrymen, or human race in general, I considered them as they really were, Yahoos[21] in shape and disposition, only a little more civilized, and qualified with the gift of speech, but making no other use of reason than to improve and multiply those vices whereof their brethren in this country had only the share that nature allotted them. When I happened to behold the reflection of my own form in a lake or fountain, I turned away my face in horror and detestation of myself, and could better endure the sight of a common Yahoo, than of my own person. By conversing with the Houyhnhnms,[22] and looking upon them with delight, I fell to imitate their gait and gesture, which is now grown into a habit, and my friends often tell me in a blunt way that I 'trot like a horse;' which, however, I take for a great compliment: neither shall I disown, that in speaking I am apt to fall into the voice and manner of the Houyhnhnms, and hear myself ridiculed on that account without the least mortification....

His name was Pedro de Mendez,[23] he was a very courteous and generous person; he entreated me to give some account of myself, and desired to know what I would eat or drink; said, I should be used as well as himself, and spoke so many obliging things, that I wondered to find such civilities from a Yahoo. However, I remained silent and sullen; I was ready to faint at the

18. cogitation: plan, thought
19. kennel: gutter in the street
20. vulgar: common people
21. Yahoos: wild, beastlike humans that Gulliver has learned to hate

22. Houyhnhnms: horse like beings who live entirely by reason, without emotion or warmth
23. Pedro de Mendez: the captain of the ship that has rescued Gulliver after the horse beings sent him out to sea

very smell of him and his men. At last I desired something to eat out of my own canoe; but he ordered me a chicken and some excellent wine, and then directed that I should be put to bed in a very clean cabin. I would not undress myself, but lay on the bedclothes, and in half an hour stole out, when I thought the crew was at dinner, and getting to the side of the ship was going to leap into the sea, and swim for my life, rather than continue among Yahoos. But one of the seamen prevented me, and having informed the captain, I was chained to my cabin.

As soon as I entered the house, my wife took me in her arms, and kissed me, at which, having not been used to the touch of that odious animal for so many years, I fell in a swoon for almost an hour. At the time I am writing it is five years since my last return to England: during the first year I could not endure my wife or children in my presence, the very smell of them was intolerable, much less could I suffer them to eat in the same room. To this hour they dare not presume to touch my bread, or drink out of the same cup, neither was I ever able to let one of them take me by the hand. The first money I laid out was to buy two young stone-horses,[24] which I keep in a good stable, and next to them the groom[25] is my greatest favourite; for I feel my spirits revived by the smell he contracts in the stable. My horses understand me tolerably well; I converse with them at least four hours every day. They are strangers to bridle or saddle; they live in great amity[26] with me, and friendship to each other.

**Write the letter for the correct answer.**

3.25    In Part IV Gulliver tries to imitate _____ .

   a. the Yahoos
   b. the Houyhnhnms
   c. Pedro de Mendez
   d. his wife

3.26    Upon his return home, Gulliver _____ .

   a. rejoiced at the sight and touch of his wife and children
   b. was indifferent towards his family
   c. loved himself so much that he neglected his family
   d. was sickened by the sight, touch, and smell of his family

3.27    Gulliver is not able to respond to Pedro de Mendez's help because _____ .

   a. de Mendez has been an old enemy
   b. de Mendez quarantines Gulliver from the sailors
   c. de Mendez was not generous at first
   d. de Mendez looks and smells like a Yahoo

**Complete this activity**

3.28    On a separate sheet of paper, tell how Gulliver's discovery of all man's corruption has or has not helped him to deal with individual men.

**Adult Check**    _____
                   Initial        Date

24.   stone-horses: stallions
25.   groom: a boy in charge of horses
26.   amity: friendship

Review the material in this section in preparation for the Self Test. This Self Test will check your mastery of this particular section as well as your knowledge of all the previous sections.

## SELF TEST 3

**Answer** *true* **or** *false* (each answer, 1 point).

3.01 _____ A simile is a comparison using like or as.

3.02 _____ An alliteration is a story in which things represent parts of a doctrine or theme.

3.03 _____ A sonnet is a ten-line poem without a rhyme scheme.

3.04 _____ Alexander Pope was born a Roman Catholic.

3.05 _____ Pope used the heroic couplet frequently to narrate, to present realistic conversation, to give memorable statements, or to give short satiric barbs.

3.06 _____ Jonathan Swift was an ordained Anglican clergyman.

3.07 _____ Swift showed his Irish patriotism by writing about starvation and the devaluation of coins in Ireland.

3.08 _____ Swift's satire which tells of three brothers' coats is *The Dunciad*.

3.09 _____ Swift wrote for the Tories.

3.010 _____ The Houyhnhnms in *Gulliver's Travels* often represent English political figures.

**Match these items** (each answer, 2 points).

3.011 _____ giving the appearance of saying one thing while meaning something else

3.012 _____ a group of writers satirizing society

3.013 _____ two rhyming lines of verse with five iambic feet

3.014 _____ beings with a wise king

3.015 _____ beings controlled by cold reason

a. Brobdingnagians

b. Yahoos

c. irony

d. heroic couplet

e. Houyhnhnms

f. Scriblerus Club

**Write the letter of the correct answer** (each answer, 2 points).

3.016 Which item did not influence Milton's writing? _____

    a. his blindness
    b. his Puritan background
    c. his friend's death
    d. his friendship with Charles II

3.017 What is the main idea of "On the Morning of Christ's Nativity"? _____

    a. that Jesus gave up heaven to live as a man
    b. that oracles say false things
    c. that Milton did not accept his blindness
    d. that Satan was ambitious and jealous

3.018 In the line, "They also serve who only stand and wait," from Milton's sonnet "On His Blindness," Milton means _____ .

    a. not everyone has to be active to do God's will

    b. standing and waiting serves no purpose

    c. serving God is more important than standing and waiting

    d. blindness prevents standing and waiting

3.019 How are Bunyan's characters in *Pilgrim's Progress* more than just symbols? _____ .

    a. They represent abstract steps in the process of salvation.

    b. They have names such as Christian, Hope, and Ignorance.

    c. They are individuals described with realistic details.

    d. They do not belong in the story.

3.020 The steam-powered inventions of the 1750s marked the beginning of the _____ .

    a. Glorious Revolution

    b. Industrial Revolution

    c. Commonwealth

    d. Restoration

3.021 A satirist may make a subject ridiculous by _____ .

    a. describing it carefully

    b. underlining it with red pencil

    c. giving it human characteristics

    d. comparing it to something undignified

3.022 Jonathan Swift _____ .

    a. hated individual men but loved powerful groups

    b. feared both individual men and powerful groups

    c. feared powerful political groups but believed that individual men can be reasonable and responsible

    d. believed that all men are as reasonable as Houyhnhnms

3.023 Swift satirizes contemporary professional men when he has the king of Brobdingnag observe that _____ .

    a. most men are not educated enough for their positions

    b. most men do not have the moral abilities required for their jobs

    c. most men dislike their jobs

    d. most men are perfectly suitable for their jobs

3.024 The inhabitants of the floating island of Laputa represent _____ .

    a. people whose studies and ideas are too abstract

    b. people who are corrupt politically

    c. people who behave like horses

    d. people who are sixty feet tall

3.025 The Houyhnhnms _____ .

    a. help Gulliver to accept himself as he is

    b. cause Gulliver to hate himself and other humans

    c. improve Gulliver's character

    d. cause Gulliver to be patient with people's problems

**Complete these sentences** (each answer, 3 points).

3.026 A long narrative poem in an elevated style with a hero and episodes important to a nation or race is an _____ .

3.027 A story in which things represent parts of a doctrine or theme is an _____ .

3.028 The 1649–1660 government that had no king was the _____ .

3.029 Something that stands for something else is a _____ .

3.030 To give something human characteristics is to _____ it.

3.031 The enlarged human features of _____ remind Gulliver of man's corruption.

3.032 When Swift gives the time, lengths of time, thorough descriptions, and Gulliver's emotional reactions, he is giving the reader _____ to make the travel account seem convincing.

3.033 In Swift's satire of the Lilliputians, the Emperor and Flimnap represent specific people, but they also represent _____ .

3.034 Flimnap the Treasurer being compared to a tight-rope walker is an example of satirizing by comparing the satirized object to something _____ .

3.035 The king of Brobdingnag compares the Englishmen that Gulliver describes to _____

_____ .

3.036 Two of Swift's pro-Irish writings were a. _____ , which encouraged the boycott of English copper coins, and b. _____

_____ , which drew attention to starvation in Ireland.

**Answer these questions** (each answer, 5 points).

3.037 In *Paradise Lost* why is Adam finally willing to leave Eden? _____

_____

_____

3.038 In *Pilgrim's Progress* what does the character Christian represent? _____

_____

3.039 In *Gulliver's Travels* what in the king of Brobdingnag's criticism makes you think that Swift was satirizing his own society? _____

_____

_____

3.040 Why do the Laputans' attentions have to be gotten by using a flapper? _____

_____

_____

_____

3.041 When Gulliver is repulsed by Pedro de Mendez and Gulliver's own family, what does his repulsion show about his character? _____

_____

_____

Score _____

Adult Check _____

Initial        Date

# IV. LITERATURE OF SENSIBILITY (1745-89)

As the Enclosure Acts took land away from the rural poor and the British grew stronger and recently industrialized areas became more congested with poor workers and clouds of soot, a few writers responded. Both Samuel Johnson and Oliver Goldsmith wrote for popular periodicals and even wrote longer prose works. Although they chose to write in ways that would please the ever-growing reading public, they also felt responsible for educating the public about social and moral problems. Like other writers of the period, they emphasized the importance of feelings and emotions and idealized the past perhaps because the present was beginning to seem so chaotic and void of genuine feeling. Nature became important for them, because the natural beauty of the countryside (disappearing even then) could inspire a closeness to God and to a simplicity of life that both writers felt was important. Even though their writing shows more emotion than the literature written from 1688 to 1745, their purpose was still to teach as well as to please.

## SECTION OBJECTIVES

**Review these objectives.** When you have completed this section, you should be able to:

13. Outline the major events in the life and career of Samuel Johnson.

14. Define the literary, moral, and political attitudes of Samuel Johnson.

15. Outline Oliver Goldsmith's writing career and explain some of the aspects of his style.

16. Identify and explain the historical background and sentimentality of Goldsmith's poem *The Deserted Village*.

## VOCABULARY

**Study these words** to enhance your learning success in this section.

| | | |
|---|---|---|
| apothecary | callousness | idealize |
| appeal | conventions | pedant |
| artifice | flat mouthpiece | poetic diction |
| auditory | fluid | rector |

### SAMUEL JOHNSON (1709–1784)

As essayist, poet, lexicographer, and moralist, Samuel Johnson was an important literary figure and moral force of his age. He was so influential that his friend James Boswell wrote a biography of Johnson that will undoubtedly remain one of the most entertaining biographies ever written.

**His life.** Johnson was born in 1709 and grew up in such poverty that he could afford only fourteen months at Oxford University. In later years he was also bothered by poverty (he had a large household of relatives to support) and was sometimes troubled with feelings of depression.

Johnson's wife, a woman twenty years older than he, died in 1752; her absence perhaps caused him to spend his last years in

**Samuel Johnson**

the company of other intellectuals with whom he could converse. At the age of sixty-four, he consented to take a walking tour of the Hebrides Islands west of Scotland with James Boswell. Johnson died in 1784. Although his life was not an easy one, Johnson's periodical essays (both moral and critical), his biographies of other writers, his *Dictionary*, and his conversational skill all illustrate a man whose common sense and feeling of public duty could overcome personal problems.

63

**His career.** Johnson began writing for periodicals in 1737, for *The Gentleman's Magazine*, and contributed to that publication until 1746. From 1750 to 1752, he wrote *The Rambler* essays, which had both moral themes and literary subjects. From 1758 to 1760, he wrote *The Idler* essays, nearly one hundred entertaining essays published in the newspaper *The Universal Chronicle*. During that time literary periodicals lived short lives, but Johnson edited or wrote book reviews and articles for many of them.

His own point of view usually affected the treatment of his subjects and themes in those essays. He was a practical critic who understood and respected the taste of the common, less scholarly reader. He disliked stiff **poetic diction** and thought that much of Milton's work was too lofty to enjoy. He insisted that literature present truth, that it be believable and realistic, and that it be refreshing enough to be interesting. He stressed that readers should feel pleasure as they read. His own taste had been carefully cultivated; he had read nearly everything of literary value published in English.

Johnson was also intensely moral. Several of his *Rambler* essays have religious themes; he was a devout Christian and believed that God's control is essential to prevent universal chaos. In a similar way, he was a Tory who preferred to be controlled by a king rather than a Parliament, whose members would undoubtedly struggle for personal, as opposed to national, advantage.

Finally, in spite of Johnson's condemnation of his own laziness, he was an energetic man. In 1755 he published a two-volume dictionary, *A Dictionary of the English Language*, which fixed the spelling of eighteenth-century English, used quotations as illustrations of usage, and defined words precisely. Immediately, the *Dictionary* was popular because it helped the rising middle class to establish correctness in word usage and spelling. He also published, in 1779 and 1781, his biographies of fifty-two writers, The *Lives of the English Poets*, in which he gave details of the writers' lives and evaluated their work. He was a conversationalist who talked with some of the most noteworthy English thinkers of that period; and he was a member of the Literary Club, a group founded in 1764 to meet once a week and discuss issues. He was a poet whose poem *The Vanity of Human Wishes*, published in 1749, has the same theme as his novel-like work *Rasselas*, published in 1759. *Rasselas*, hastily written to make money to pay for his mother's funeral expenses, emphasizes the impossibility of complete happiness. If Johnson himself was not happy, he was at least contributing toward the pleasure and education of others.

**Write the letter of the correct answer.**

4.1    James Boswell wrote _____ .

   a. essays for *The Rambler*
   b. chapters for a dictionary
   c. a biography of Johnson
   d. periodical notices for the Literary Club

4.2    Samuel Johnson did *not* write _____ .

   a. poetry
   b. a story about himself, describing his happiness
   c. periodical essays in several newspapers
   d. a dictionary in two volumes

4.3  As a literary critic, Johnson disliked _____.

    a. literature that is believable and realistic

    b. literature with unique, refreshing elements

    c. literature with elaborate poetic diction

    d. literature that would appeal to the common reader

4.4  Johnson's political views were nearest those of _____ .

    a. a Tory

    b. a Whig

    c. an anarchist

    d. a socialist

**Complete these statements.**

4.5  One periodical in which Johnson's essays appeared was _____

_____ .

4.6  One longer work that Johnson published was _____

_____ .

## OLIVER GOLDSMITH (1730–1774)

Oliver Goldsmith and Samuel Johnson were friends for good reasons; they shared many of the same ideas, did many of the same types of writing jobs, and wrote for the same reasons: to ease their own poverty and to instruct and please the reading public. Both were members of the Literary Club, both were Tories who distrusted wealthy members of Parliament and preferred a strong monarchy instead, and both admired the disciplined writing of Pope and Swift. Yet Goldsmith's works are more entertaining than Johnson's writing, which tends to teach more than to please. Goldsmith was so skillful at pleasing by touching emotions and **idealizing** simple scenes that he often taught without the reader being aware that instruction can accompany pleasure.

**Oliver Goldsmith**

**His life.** Goldsmith's early life is a story of poverty and missed opportunities. He was probably born in 1730 in Ireland, the son of a **rector** of a small church. He would always remain embarrassed by his Irish dialect and his poverty and would be self-conscious and self-critical. He failed to continue his studies both of law and medicine, and he was turned down for ordination in the Church of England. From 1756 on, he spent several years trying different ways to earn a living: acting, assisting an **apothecary**, doctoring in the slums, proofreading, teaching, reviewing, and translating. If all these attempts did not enable him to support himself comfortably, however, they did teach him much about human nature and caused him to write clearly and entertainingly, without a stiff, scholarly style.

In the 1750s a need for periodical writers arose, and Goldsmith's flexibility helped to fill that need. From 1757 to 1762, Goldsmith contributed to at least ten periodicals. During 1759 when he published *An Enquiry into the Present State of Polite Learning in Europe*, he was also contributing to the periodical *The Bee*. From 1760 to 1761, *the Citizen of the World* essays, in the form of letters from a Chinese traveler in London to home, appeared in *The Public Ledger*. In this series he satirized present-day society by using the detached Chinese observer. He emphasized his beliefs that customs are relative, that one should be tolerant of the customs of other nations, and that simplicity is always best. Characters he introduced in his series are not **flat mouthpieces**, however. He used realistic details to present characters he liked. Throughout these essays, his style remains entertaining and clear. He has been called one of the most readable writers of his century because his writing is so vivid and **fluid**. His personality in the essays is thoroughly likable; he refused to be the **pedant** as Johnson sometimes was. He was not a complete sentimentalist losing himself in emotions, but he was too sympathetic to be a consistent satirist.

Goldsmith was also a popular poet, dramatist, and novelist. In 1764 he published his poem *The Traveler*, which states several of his themes, especially on excesses and happiness. He wrote that everything—wealth, commerce, honor, liberty, contentment—has a happiness that, if carried to excess, can produce unhappiness. As a poet, he believed that poetry should instruct as well as please and should be addressed to the public rather than to those few readers seeking scholarly pleasure. He thought that poetry should convey strong emotions and that its form and language should be appropriate to the message. Like his predecessors he used couplets and broad moral themes and addressed his poems to educated men everywhere. He used poetic **conventions** such as poetic diction and personification, but his poetry had a new, emotional quality in a more straightforward language. In 1770, he published his most famous poem, *The Deserted Village*, **appealing** against the injustices and materialism of the age.

In 1766, to pay his debt to his landlady, he published the novel *The Vicar of Wakefield*. The plot is very involved. It begins with the members of a happy parson's family enjoying the beauties of the rural countryside. Through their greed to make wealthy matches for their daughters, however, they end up in prison and in disgrace. The Primrose family must learn the danger of false appearances, the evils of ambition, and the importance of moral strength before they can be released from their earthly prison. Goldsmith probed the horrors of prison life and satirized ambitious females even as he heaped sentiment into his happy conclusion.

His play, *She Stoops to Conquer*, was written in 1771 and produced in 1773. The less successful play, *The Good Natured Man*, had been produced in 1768. In 1774 he died of a fever from a bladder infection and from worry over a two-thousand-pound debt according to his friend Joshua Reynolds, the artist. Samuel Johnson wrote his epitaph.

**Answer** *true* **or** *false*.

| | | |
|---|---|---|
| 4.7 | _____ | Oliver Goldsmith became a wealthy doctor. |
| 4.8 | _____ | Goldsmith used a learned style that is best appreciated by those who are well educated. |
| 4.9 | _____ | From 1757 to 1762, Goldsmith contributed to at least ten periodicals. |
| 4.10 | _____ | Goldsmith believed that one should be tolerant of the customs of other nations. |
| 4.11 | _____ | Goldsmith believed that an excess of anything can lead to unhappiness. |
| 4.12 | _____ | Goldsmith wrote a poem entitled *The Traveler* which discusses excesses. |

**His poem: *The Deserted Village*.** *The Deserted Village* was one of the most popular poems in the eighteenth century. Its idealization of simple rural life and its sense of a lost past appealed to the taste for the sensitively described, emotional subjects that were popular at the time. The poem was sincerely written with a definite purpose in mind, as revealed by Goldsmith's own words in his dedication to the poem:

> "All my views and enquiries have led me to believe those miseries real, which I here attempt to display...In regretting the depopulation of the country. I inveigh against the increase of our luxuries; and here also I expect the shout of modern politicians against me."

The "depopulation of the country" of which Goldsmith spoke was the forced moving of the rural poor from the Commons, land which had been available to everyone for grazing without ownership, to recently industrialized cities. The Enclosure movement was responsible for large groups of landless, "toolless" poor going either to industrialized cities or to America for a new start. The poem also notes the beginning of industrialized slums.

Although the poem contains a new, sentimental element, it also contains many devices that Milton and Pope used. It laments the passing of an age much as Milton lamented his dead friend in *Lycidas*; thus, this poem has been called a pastoral elegy. It is written in heroic couplets, a disciplined form Pope used, and makes use of poetic diction and personification. Goldsmith has added sentiment and idealization of rural scenes to the traditional elements. His heroic couplets move slowly and thoughtfully, not at Pope's crisp pace. Finally, his structure seems less disciplined as he repeats his laments to build up emotional impact.

As you read the poem, you should keep in mind Goldsmith's central ideas; he stresses how rural self-reliance and innocence have been destroyed by greedy landowners and industrialization. At the end of the poem, the rural virtues—Toil, Care, Tenderness, Piety, Loyalty, and Love—march to the sea with the homeless poor. Even Poetry herself is driven to leave England by the **callousness** of the new age of greed. Note also Goldsmith's poetic diction in such phrases as "labouring swain" and "sheltered cot." Notice the Eden-like description of the village, especially the description of pleasing sounds (**auditory** imagery). Finally, notice how Goldsmith contrasts Nature with the **artifice** of the wealthy (Lines 251 to 264). This theme will become even more important in literature written later.

**Write the letter of the correct answer.**

4.13 Goldsmith wrote *The Deserted Village* specifically to describe the results of_____

    a. the civil war in England
    b. the plague in his native Irish village
    c. the Enclosure Acts
    d. the invention of the steam engine .

4.14 Which phrase describes the poem? _____

    a. could be called a pastoral elegy    c. contains nonpoetic diction
    b. written in blank verse    d. is satirical and emotionless

4.15 Which phrase is *not* a central idea of *The Deserted Village*? _____

    a. the destruction of self-reliance    c. the destructiveness of greed
    b. the destruction of innocence    d. the destructiveness of the sea

Lines 1–74, 83–96, 113–128, 137–180:

Sweet Auburn[1] loveliest village of the plain,
Where health and plenty cheered the labouring swain,[2]
Where smiling spring its earliest visit paid,
And parting summer's lingering blooms delayed:
Dear lovely bowers[3] of innocence and ease,
Seats of my youth, when every sport could please,
How often have I loitered o'er thy green,
Where humble happiness endeared each scene;
How often have I paused on every charm,
The sheltered cot,[4] the cultivated farm,                                    10
The never-failing brook, the busy mill,
The decent church that topped the neighbouring hill,
The hawthorn bush, with seats beneath the shade,
For talking age and whispering lovers made;
How often have I blessed the coming day,
When toil remitting lent its turn to play,
And all the village train, from labour free,
Led up their sports beneath the spreading tree;
While many a pastime circled in the shade,
The young contending as the old surveyed;                                     20
And many a gambol frolicked o'er the ground,
And sleights of art[5] and feats of strength went round;
And still as each repeated pleasure tired,
Succeeding sports the mirthful band inspired:
The dancing pair that simply sought renown,
By holding out to tire each other down;

1. Auburn: fictional name
2. labouring swain: shepherd
3 bowers: shelters made of branches

4 sheltered cot: small house
5. sleights of art: tricks or juggling

68

The swain mistrustless of his smutted face,
While secret laughter tittered round the place;
The bashful virgin's side-long looks of love,
The matron's glance that would those looks reprove:                    30
These were thy charms, sweet village; sports like these,
With sweet succession, taught e'en toil to please;
These round thy bowers their cheerful influence shed,
These were thy charms—But all these charms are fled.

    Sweet smiling village, loveliest of the lawn,
Thy sports are fled, and all thy charms withdrawn;
Amidst thy bowers the tyrant's[6] hand is seen,
And desolation saddens all thy green:
One only master grasps the whole domain,[7]
And half a tillage *stints*[8] thy smiling plain:                      40
No more thy glassy brook reflects the day,
But choked with sedges,[9] works its weedy way.
Along thy glades, a solitary guest,
The hollow-sounding bittern guards its nest;
Amidst thy desert walks the lapwing flies,
And tires their echoes with unvaried cries.
Sunk are thy bowers, in shapeless ruin all,
And the long grass o'ertops the mouldering wall;
And, trembling, shrinking from the spoiler's hand,
Far, far away, thy children leave the land.                            50

    Ill fares the land, to hastening ills a prey,
Where wealth accumulates, and men decay:
Princes and lords may flourish, or may fade;
A breath can make them, as a breath has made;
But a bold peasantry, their country's pride,
When once destroyed, can never be supplied.

    A time there was, ere England's griefs began,
When every rood[10] of ground maintained its man;
For him light labour spread her wholesome store,
Just gave what life required, but gave no more:                        60
His best companions, innocence and health;
And his best riches, ignorance of wealth.

    But times are altered; trade's unfeeling train
Usurp[11] the land and dispossess[12] the swain;
Along the lawn, where scattered hamlets rose,
Unwieldy wealth, and cumbrous[13] pomp repose;
And every want to opulence allied,
And every pang that folly pays to pride.
Those gentle hours that plenty bade to bloom,
Those calm desires that asked but little room,                         70
Those healthful sports that graced the peaceful scene,
Lived in each look, and brightened all the green;
These, far departing, seek a kinder shore,
And rural mirth and manners are no more.

. . . . . . . . . . . . . . . . . . . . . . . . . . . . . . . . .

6.  tyrants: lord who bought up the land and turned away the families
7.  one... domain: reference to Enclosure Acts (1760-64)
8.  stints: limits
9.  sedges: tufted marsh plants
10. rood: unit of land, about a quarter of an acre
11. usurp: to seize and hold
12. dispossess: to put out of occupancy
13. cumbrous: heavy

In all my wanderings round this world of care,                    83
In all my griefs—and GOD has given my share—
I still had hopes my latest hours to crown,
Amidst these humble bowers to lay me down;
To husband,[14] out life's taper at the close,
And keep the flame from wasting by repose.
I still had hopes, for pride attends us still,                    90
Amidst the swains to show my book-learned skill,
Around my fire an evening group to draw,
And tell of all I felt, and all I saw;
And, as a hare, whom hounds and horns pursue,
Pants to the place from whence at first she flew,
I still had hopes, my long vexations passed,
Here to return—and die at home at last.

. . . . . . . . . . . . . . . . . . . . . . . . . . . . . . . . . .

Sweet was the sound when oft at evening's close                   113
Up yonder hill the village murmur rose;
There, as I passed with careless steps and slow,
The mingling notes came softened from below;
The swain responsive as the milk-maid sung,
The sober herd that lowed to meet their young:
The noisy geese that gabbled o'er the pool,
The playful children just let loose from school;                  120
The watchdog's voice that bayed the whisp'ring wind,
And the loud laugh that spoke the vacant mind;
These all in sweet confusion sought the shade,
And filled each pause the nightingale had made.
But now the sounds of population fail,
No cheerful murmurs fluctuate in the gale,
No busy steps the grass-grown footway tread,
For all the bloomy flush of life is fled.

. . . . . . . . . . . . . . . . . . . . . . . . . . . . . . . . . .

Near yonder copse,[15] where once the garden smiled,             137
And still where many a garden flower grows wild;
There, where a few torn shrubs the place disclose,
The village preacher's modest mansion rose.                      140
A man he was to all the country dear,
And passing rich with forty pounds a year;
Remote from towns he ran his godly race,
Nor e'er had changed, nor wished to change his place;
Unpractised he to fawn, or seek for power,
By doctrines fashioned to the varying hour;
Far other aims his heart had learned to prize,
More skilled to raise the wretched than to rise.
His house was known to all the vagrant train,
He chid[16] their wanderings, but relieved their pain;           150
The long remembered beggar was his guest;
Whose beard descending swept his aged breast;
The ruined spendthrift, now no longer proud,
Claimed kindred there, and had his claims allowed;
The broken soldier, kindly bade[17] to stay,

14. husband to manage prudently, to conserve        16. chid: spoke out against
15. copse: thicket growth of small trees            17. bade: invited

Sat by his fire, and talked the night away;
Wept o'er his wounds, or tales of sorrow done,
Shouldered his crutch, and showed how fields were won.
Pleased with his guests, the good man learned to glow,
And quite forgot their vices in their woe;          160
Careless their merits, or their faults to scan,
His pity gave ere[18] charity began.

     Thus to relieve the wretched was his pride,
And e'en his failings leaned to Virtue's side;
But in his duty prompt at every call,
He watched and wept, he prayed and felt for all.
And, as a bird each fond endearment tries
To tempt its new-fledged offspring to the skies,
He tried each art, reproved each dull delay,
Allured to brighter worlds, and led the way.          170

     Beside the bed where parting life was laid,
And sorrow, guilt, and pain, by turns dismayed,
The reverend champion stood. At his control
Despair and anguish fled the struggling soul;
Comfort came down the trembling wretch to raise.
And his last faltering accents whispered praise.

     At church, with meek and unaffected grace,
His looks adorned the venerable place;
Truth from his lips prevailed the double sway,
And fools, who came to scoff, remained to pray.          180

**Write the letter of the correct answer.**

4.16 What are the phrases "labouring swain," "sheltered cot," and "mirthful band" examples of? _____ .

  a. personification              c. poetic diction
  b. simile                       d. heroic couplet

4.17 What is "smiling spring" an example of? _____ .

  a. personification              c. poetic diction
  b. simile                       d. heroic couplet

4.18 Line 47 mentions bowers ("Sunk are thy bowers in shapeless ruin all"); the term is repeated in Line 5 ("Dear lovely bowers of innocence and ease"). Why does the poet repeat this image? _____ .

  a. because he cannot think of anything else
  b. because he wants to contrast the present loss with the idealized past
  c. because bowers are always around
  d. because he wants to emphasize trees

4.19 Reread Lines 51–56. What do they mean? _____ .

  a. Rich men come and go, but farmers cannot be replaced.
  b. Rich men suffocate easily and peasants always want something.
  c. Wealth lasts forever while men decay.
  d. Princes should never be allowed to fade.

18. ere: before

**4.20**  Reread Lines 83–96. What role does the poet himself play? _____ .

  a. He had hoped to find his friends still living.
  b. He had hoped to retire in the village and die there.
  c. He had experienced many griefs there.
  d. He had met his wife there.

**4.21**  What does Goldsmith achieve as he describes the village preacher in the line "He watched and wept, he prayed and felt, for all"? _____ .

  a. the sentimental portrait of a man who did many things
  b. the sentimental portrait of a man whose emotions were easily aroused who is therefore worthy of respect
  c. the sentimental portrait of a man who couldn't stop crying
  d. the portrait of a confused man

**Answer these questions.**

**4.22**  What is the meaning of the simile in Lines 93–96? _____

_____

_____

**4.23**  What are some of the sounds described in Lines 113–126? _____

_____

_____

Lines 251–186, 303–344, 363–370, 395–410, 423–430:

> Yes! let the rich deride, the proud disdain,  251
> These simple blessings of the lowly train;
> To me more dear, congenial to my heart,
> One native charm, than all the gloss of art;
> Spontaneous joys, where nature has its play,
> The soul adopts, and owns their first-born sway;
> Lightly they frolic o'er the vacant mind,
> Unenvied, unmolested, unconfined:
> But the long pomp, the midnight masquerade,
> With all the freaks of wanton wealth arrayed,  260
> In these, ere triflers half their wish obtain,
> The toiling pleasure sickens into pain;
> And, e'en while fashion's brightest arts decoy,
> The heart distrusting asks, if this be joy.
>
> Ye friends to truth, ye statesmen, who survey,
> The rich man's joys increase, the poor's decay,
> 'Tis yours to judge, how wide the limits stand
> Between a splendid and a happy land.
> Proud swells the tide with loads of freighted ore,[19]
> And shouting Folly hails them from her shore;  270
> Hoards, e'en beyond the miser's wish abound,
> And rich men flock from all the world around.
> Yet count our gains. This wealth is but a name
> That leaves our useful products still the same.

19.  loads. . . ore: steam-driven ships with coal

Not so the loss. The man of wealth and pride
Takes up a space that many poor supplied;
Space for his lake, his park's extended bounds,
Space for his horses, equipage, and hounds;
The robe that wraps his limbs in silken sloth
Has robbed the neighbouring fields of half their growth,          280
His seat, where solitary sports are seen,
Indignant spurns[20] the cottage from the green;
Around the world each needful product flies,
For all the luxuries the world supplies:
While thus the land adorned for pleasure, all
In barren splendour feebly waits the fall.

. . . . . . . . . . . . . . . . . . . . . . . . . . . . . . . . .

Where then, ah! where, shall poverty reside,                      303
To 'scape the pressure of contiguous[21] pride?
If to some common's fenceless limits strayed,
He drives his flock to pick the scanty blade,
Those fenceless fields the sons of wealth divide,
And e'en the bare-worn common[22] is denied.

If to the city sped—What waits him there?
To see profusion[23] that he must not share;                     310
To see ten thousand baneful[24] arts combined
To pamper luxury, and thin mankind;
To see those joys the sons of pleasure know
Extorted from his fellow creature's woe.
Here, while the courtier glitters in brocade,
There the pale artist plies the sickly trade;
Here, while the proud their long-drawn pomps display,
There the black gibbet[25] glooms beside the way.
The dome where Pleasure holds her midnight reign
Here richly decks, admits the gorgeous train;                     320
Tumultuous grandeur crowds the blazing square,
The rattling chariots clash, the torches glare.
Sure scenes like these no troubles e'er annoy)
Sure these denote one universal joy!
Are these thy serious thoughts?—Ah, turn shine eyes
Where the poor houseless shiv'ring female lies.
She once, perhaps, in village plenty blessed,
Has wept at tales of innocence distressed,
Her modest looks the cottage might adorn,
Sweet as the primrose peeps beneath the thorn;                    330
Now lost to all; her friends, her virtue fled,
Near her betrayer's door she lays her head,
And, pinched with cold, and shrinking from the shower,
With heavy heart deplores that luckless hour,
When idly first, ambitious of the town,
She left her wheel[26] and robes of country brown.

Do shine, sweet AUBURN, shine, the loveliest train,
Do thy fair tribes participate[27] her pain?
E'en now, perhaps, by cold and hunger led,
At proud men's doors they ask a little bread!                     340

---

20.  spurns: displaces
21.  contiguous: immediately following
22.  common: land once public property
23.  profusion: an abundance, an extravagant

24.  baneful: creating destruction
25.  gibbet: post for hanging executed criminals
26.  wheel: spinning wheel
27.  participate: share

Ah, no. To distant climes,[28] a dreary scene,
Where half the convex world intrudes between,
Through torrid[29] tracts with fainting steps they go,
Where wild Altama[30] murmurs to their woe.

. . . . . . . . . . . . . . . . . . . . . . . . . . . . . . . . . . . .

Good Heaven! what sorrows gloomed that parting day,                363
That called them from their native walks away;
When the poor exiles, every pleasure past,
Hung round their bowers, and fondly looked their last,
And took a long farewell, and wished in vain
For seats like these beyond the western main;
And shuddering still to face the distant deep,
Returned and wept, and still returned to weep.                     370

. . . . . . . . . . . . . . . . . . . . . . . . . . . . . . . . . . . .

E'en now the devastation is begun,                                 395
And half the business of destruction done;
E'en now, methinks, as pondering here I stand,
I see the rural virtues leave the land:
Down where yon anchoring vessel spreads the sail,
That idly waiting flaps with every gale,                           400
Downward they move, a melancholy band,
Pass from the shore, and darken all the strand[31]
Contented toil, and hospitable care,
And kind connubial[32] tenderness, are there;
And piety with wishes placed above,
And steady loyalty, and faithful love.
And thou, sweet Poetry, thou loveliest maid,
Still first to fly where sensual joys invade;
Unfit in these degenerate times of shame,
To catch the heart, or strike for honest fame;                    410

. . . . . . . . . . . . . . . . . . . . . . . . . . . . . . . . . . . .

...with thy persuasive strain                                      423
Teach erring man to spurn[33] the rage of gain;
Teach him, that states of native strength possessed,
Though very poor, may still be very blessed;
That trade's proud empire hastes to swift decay,
As ocean sweeps the laboured mole[34] away;
While self-dependent power can time defy,
As rocks resist the billows and the sky.                          430

---

28.  climes: climates
29.  torrid: scorching
30.  **Altama**: river in Georgia (an allusion to the fact the poor go to America)
31.  strand: shore
32.  connubial: related to marriage, joined
33.  spurn: to reject with disdain
34.  mole: pier, land.

**Write the letter of the correct answer.**

4.24 What is the contrast presented in Lines 251–264? _____ .

    a. between spontaneous joys and native charm

    b. between wanton wealth and the gloss of art

    c. between man's artifice and Nature's spontaneity

    d. between the pure soul and Nature's spontaneity

4.25 What movements are described in Lines 269–286? _____ .

    a. increased trade with other countries and the enclosure of land

    b. the Industrial Revolution and the Commonwealth

    c. the stock market and taxation

    d. the agricultural revolution and the Commonwealth

4.26 Reread Lines 309–326. What is the tone (attitude of Goldsmith toward the subject) in **Lines 323 and 324?** _____ .

    a. He is sincere.

    b. He is being ironic; he doesn't mean what he says.

    c. He does not approve of joy.

    d. He is praising city wealth.

4.27 Poetry must leave England with the displaced villagers and the rural virtues because _____ .

    a. the common people are uneducated and therefore cannot read poetry

    b. all the great poets are dead

    c. the hearts of the people have been so corrupted that they cannot appreciate poetry

    d. the work loads created by the Industrial Revolution allow no time for the reading of poetry

4.28 According to Lines 423–430, the function of poetry is to _____ .

    a. teach people to live simple, unambitious lives

    b. encourage patriotism and empire-building

    c. inspire people to use their material wealth as a stepping-stone to happiness

    d. encourage the destruction of cities and the restoration of farm lands

**Complete this activity.**

4.29 Both Goldsmith and Swift condemned the evils of their age, but they sometimes attacked different things and used different approaches. On separate sheets of paper, write a three-page essay comparing (finding similarities) or contrasting (finding differences) their attacks. Begin your paper with one statement that summarizes how these two authors are being compared or contrasted. Follow this introduction with your supporting argument made up of reasons and examples to make the comparison or contrast clear. Before you begin to write your own paper, write an outline. Arrange your argument by points of comparison (or contrast). For example, if you decide that both authors are alike in their condemnation of stray dogs and lice, you will first discuss how Swift deals with dogs; then, how Goldsmith does. After that point is dealt with, you will discuss how Swift deals with lice; and then, how Goldsmith does. This approach is called an alternating method. Pay close attention to paragraph and sentence structure.

Adult Check     _____
                      Initial      Date

Before you take this last Self Test, you may want to do one or more of these self checks.

1. _____ Read the objectives. Determine if you can do them.

2. _____ Restudy the material related to any objectives that you cannot do.

3. _____ Use the SQ3R study procedure to review the material:
   a. **S**can the sections.
   b. **Q**uestion yourself again (review the questions you wrote initially).
   c. **R**ead to answer your questions.
   d. **R**ecite the answers to yourself.
   e. **R**eview areas you didn't understand.

4. _____ Review all vocabulary, activities, and Self Tests, writing a correct answer for each wrong answer.

## SELF TEST 4

**Answer** *true* **or** *false* (each answer, 1 point).

4.01 _____ Charles II was restored to the throne in 1660.

4.02 _____ The Puritans believed that the Anglican Church was corrupted by unnecessary ritual and by an organization that was no longer able to reach each member, and that it was controlled by a corrupt government and monarchy.

4.03 _____ Periodicals and the novel became less popular as the more powerful middle class began to read.

4.04 _____ When public land was enclosed for private estates, the rural poor were forced to go either to recently industrialized areas or to America.

4.05 _____ Milton was imprisoned because he owed money.

4.06 _____ John Bunyan studied the Bible carefully after the civil war in England.

4.07 _____ James Boswell wrote a biography of Oliver Goldsmith.

4.08 _____ Samuel Johnson thought that literature should appeal to the common reader and should teach as well as please.

4.09 _____ Samuel Johnson wrote periodical essays in several newspapers.

4.010 _____ Oliver Goldsmith believed that one can never be too rich.

4.011 _____ In *The Deserted Village*, Goldsmith has little respect for the sentimental village preacher.

**Write the letter of the correct answer** (each answer, 2 points).

4.012 What was *not* happening in the second half of the eighteenth century? _____
   a. the "agricultural revolution"       c. a growing British Empire
   b. the Industrial Revolution           d. decreased trade with other countries

4.013 In "On the Morning of Christ's Nativity," what did Christ forsake and what did He choose? _____
   a. He left God's side to be alone in the wilderness.
   b. He left Mary's side to turn water into wine.
   c. He left heaven to live in darkness as a mortal.
   d. He left the "darksome earth" to join His Father.

76

4.014 In "On His Blindness," Milton regrets _____ .

    a. that his blindness restricts his work
    b. that he is blind
    c. that he is in prison
    d. that God is so unfair

4.015 *Pilgrim's Progress* is about _____ .

    a. a man who fights for William III
    b. a man whose land is enclosed
    c. a man who drowns in the River of Death
    d. a man who saves his soul

4.016 Jonathan Swift satirized contemporary professional men in *Gulliver's Travels* when he had the king of Brobdingnag observe that _____ .

    a. most men dislike their jobs
    b. most men aren't educated enough for their positions
    c. most men are not morally suitable for their jobs
    d. most men are perfectly suitable for their jobs

4.017 Samuel Johnson did not publish _____ .

    a. *A Dictionary of the English Language*
    b. *The Vicar of Wakefield*
    c. *The Lives of the English Poets*
    d. *Rasselas*

4.018 What is the career Goldsmith did *not* attempt? _____

    a. to be a member of Parliament
    b. to be a doctor
    c. to be a lawyer
    d. to be a clergyman

4.019 Goldsmith did *not* write _____ .

    a. a poem entitled *The Traveler* about excesses
    b. a novel entitled *The Vicar of Wakefield* about a parson's family
    c. a short-story entitled *The Deserted Vicar*
    d. a play entitled She *Stoops to Conquer*

4.020 In *The Deserted Village*, Poetry's walking to the sea (because people left in England are too corrupted by wealth to appreciate art), is an example of _____ .

    a. personification
    b. simile
    c. poetic diction
    d. heroic couplet

4.021 In *The Deserted Village* the poet says that _____ .

    a. rich men suffocate easily and peasants always want something
    b. rich men come and go, but farmers can't be replaced
    c. wealth lasts forever, while men decay
    d. princes should never be allowed to rule

**Complete these sentences** (each answer, 3 points).

4.022    A poem with fourteen lines, of either the Italian or English type, is a _____.

4.023    A comparison using "like" or "as" is a _____.

4.024    The repetition of initial consonants is called _____.

4.025    A story in which things represent parts of a doctrine or theme is an _____.

4.026    A _____ consists of two rhyming lines of verse with five iambic feet.

4.027    When one gives the appearance of saying one thing while meaning something else, _____ is used.

4.028    If a writer ridicules something by exaggerating its corruption, placing it next to something undignified, or giving it false praise, he is _____ it.

4.029    Johnson's and Goldsmith's political views were nearest those of a _____.

4.030    Goldsmith wrote *The Deserted Village* to describe the results of the _____ Acts.

4.031    When Goldsmith laments the loss of the villagers in *The Deserted Village* and stresses the village preacher's sympathy with his congregation, Goldsmith is using _____

_____

4.032    In *The Deserted Village* the phrases, "laboring swain," "sheltered cot," and "mirthful land," are examples of _____.

**Match these items that explain some of Swift's satire in** *Gulliver's Travels* (each answer, 2 points).

4.033    _____    represent George I
4.034    _____    directly criticizes the English way of life
4.035    _____    represents abstract thinkers in England

a. Houyhnhnms
b. Laputans
c. Emperor of the Lilliputians
d. king of the Brobdingnagians

**Answer these questions** (each numbered answer, 5 points).

4.036    What are five of the political, economic, or cultural events in the seventeenth or eighteenth centuries that influenced social unrest?

a. _____

b. _____

c. _____

d. _____

e. _____

4.037    In *Paradise Lost* why is Adam finally willing to leave Eden? _____

_____

4.038    In *Pilgrim's Progress* how are Bunyan's characters more than just symbols? _____

_____

4.039    List two activities in Swift's life that were either political or religious or both and that reflected in his satire.

a. _____

b. _____

4.040 Explain these three aspects of *The Deserted Village*.

a. Why is the village deserted? _____

_____

b. Where are the villagers now forced to go? _____

_____

c. How does the poet personally emphasize the loss of the village? _____

_____

_____

| 76 |
|----|
| 95 |

Score _____

Adult Check _____

Initial          Date

---

Before taking the LIFEPAC Test, you may want to do one or more of these self checks.
1. _____    Read the objectives. Check to see if you can do them.
2. _____    Restudy the material related to any objectives that you cannot do.
3. _____    Use the SQ3R study procedure to review the material.
4. _____    Review activities, Self Tests, and LIFEPAC vocabulary words.
5. _____    Restudy areas of weakness indicated by the last Self Test.

---

## GLOSSARY

**apothecary.** One preparing and selling drugs; in the eighteenth century he also practiced medicine.

**appeal.** To arouse a sympathetic response.

**artifice.** Trickery.

**auditory.** Experienced by hearing.

**barb.** A biting or critical remark.

**beau.** A man who frequently escorts a woman.

**burlesque.** A mockery by exaggerated literary imitation.

**callousness.** Hardness, lack of emotion.

**cleric.** A member of the clergy.

**contemplative.** Given to a concentration on spiritual or abstract things.

**conventions.** Rules or practices of conduct or behavior.

**digression.** A turning aside from the main point.

**displaced.** Forced from home.

**dissenter.** One that holds a different opinion, such as an English Nonconformist.

**effeminate.** Unmanly.

**elevated** On a high plane morally or intellectually.

**emigrate.** To leave a home to live elsewhere.

**episode.** A brief unit of action; an incident.

**exclusive.** Limiting use to a single group or individual; single, whole.

**flat mouthpiece.** A character illustrating a single idea or quality; never surprises the reader with variety

**fluid.** Having a smooth, easy style

**idealize.** To form ideals.

**inflated.** Puffed up, filled up (with pride or air).

**intimate.** To suggest.

**invocation.** Act of calling for help, act of legal enforcement.

**lyrical.** Suitable for music, expressing intense emotion, unrestrained.

**maneuver.** To scheme, to trick.

**misanthrope.** A person who hates or distrusts all people.

**Muse.** A source of inspiration; one of nine sisters, goddesses in Greek mythology, who inspired man's inventions.

**nonconformist.** A person who does not conform to the Church of England.

**parish.** A local church community, an area committed to one pastor.

**pastoral elegy.** A poem using imagery, usually used to describe country life; it is dignified and serious, and often expresses grief at the loss of a friend.

**pedant.** One who parades his learning.

**periodical.** Something published with a fixed interval between issues or numbers.

**pilgrim.** One who journeys to another land; one who travels to a holy shrine.

**poetic diction.** Words chosen for poetry that are different from those used for speech; they are usually older words that sometimes contain comparisons and do not name something directly.

**propagandist.** One who spreads ideas to help an institution.

**rational.** Having reason, based on reasoning.

**rector.** A clergyman in charge of a parish.

**sensibility.** Use of emotionalism as opposed to rationalism.

**sentimental.** Overly emotional, giving enjoyment at the expense of emotions, and idealizing human nature

**suppressive.** Tending to put down, keeping from public knowledge.

**theme.** The central idea in a literary work.

**universal.** Covering without limit or exception, occurring everywhere.

**vulnerability.** Being easily attacked, damaged, or hurt.